HAR

GW00597710

Standoff at Liberty

When Special Investigator Frank Angel rides into the town of Liberty in pursuit of fugitive outlaw Harry Culp, he little realizes that he will soon be fighting for his life. His danger comes not from Culp, but from the corrupt Judge Cranford and Liberty's Sheriff Sherman, together with his sinister deputies.

Unknown to Angel, the outlaw has already been murdered on the orders of Cranford and his stolen loot appropriated. Angel soon falls foul of the deputies when he stops them from harassing a young woman, only to find himself framed and sentenced to six months' hard labour in the prison camp run by Cranford's sadistic henchmen.

Will he follow the dead outlaw to Boot Hill?

Standoff at Liberty

Daniel Rockfern

A Black Horse Western

ROBERT HALE · LONDON

© Frederick Nolan 2004
First published in Great Britain 2004

ISBN 0 7090 7632 0

Robert Hale Limited
Clerkenwell House
Clerkenwell Green
London EC1R 0HT

Typeset by
Derek Doyle & Associates in Liverpool.
Printed and bound in Great Britain by
Antony Rowe Limited, Wiltshire

1

'She's lying!' Harry Culp protested wildly. 'I never laid a finger on her!'

The girl, lacquered red hair tumbling around her white shoulders, flung out a slim arm, a long finger pointing accusingly at Culp.

'He did so too!' she wailed, red mouth puckering. 'He . . . he was going to force me to—'

'Force you? Hell, that's all. . . .' Culp yelled.

One of the hard-faced deputies reached out and prodded Culp's shoulder. He was a big man, built like the side of a house, and the power in his large fist shoved Culp across the alley. The other deputy who had placed himself behind Culp, stuck out a foot. Culp tripped and fell, sprawling on his back in the dirt of the gloomy alley. He lay stunned, staring up at the menacing shapes of the two deputies. A protest rose in his throat, and died just as swiftly. Something warned him to be careful. There was a bad feeling beginning to grow. Harry Culp was no fool. He'd been on the wrong side of the law for long enough to know that he had walked right into a set-up. The girl was in with the two deputies. The next move would be a threat of jail ... or a demand for money. It was so obvious it might have been laughable if it hadn't been for the nagging worry at the back of Culp's mind. Maybe he'd missed something. He couldn't put his finger on it but he was certain there was more to this set-up than he'd realized.

'On your feet,' demanded the deputy who had laid Culp on his back. 'We got a place for bastards like you!'

On his feet Harry Culp brushed dirt from his clothing. He glanced at the big deputy, trying to read the expression in the man's small, mean eyes. He decided it might be best to give the game a chance to play itself out.

'All right, boys, you got me,' he said, forcing a little humour into his tone. 'Now how about us getting round to settling this right here? I reckon we can figure something out to suit us all. Even the little lady there. What's the going rate?' Culp reached slowly into his coat pocket and drew out his wallet.

The big deputy dropped his eyes to the wallet, studying it closely. After a minute he raised his head, sucking in a sharp breath. Without prior warning his large right fist came out of nowhere and hit Culp full in the mouth. Culp staggered back across the alley, his shoulders banging painfully against the rough wall of the building

6

behind him. Warm blood was oozing thickly from his mashed lips, dripping from his chin on to his shirt-front. He lifted a hand and clumsily wiped at the sticky wetness running down his face.

'This feller's got nasty habits,' the big deputy said. 'First he tries to rape the lady. Now he's trying to bribe us. Koch, we better get him over to the jail 'fore he does anything else.'

The one called Koch grinned. 'Hell, Duggan, the judge is going to love this boy!'

Duggan reached out and took Culp's arm. Then he hesitated.

'You carryin' a gun?'

Culp just nodded and opened his coat, revealing the short-barrelled Colt he wore in a shoulder rig. Duggan took the gun, tucking it in his belt.

'Never do trust a feller who keeps his gun hid,' he remarked. 'You walk ahead of me, mister, and don't try any funny stuff! One wrong move and I'll kick the shit right out of you!'

They emerged from the alley and cut across the main street. Curious bystanders gathered on the lamplit boardwalks outside the saloons and gambling-houses. Harry Culp could see the stone-built jail. It looked solid. It was going to be a lot harder getting out than it had been getting in, he thought, sourly. He didn't worry too much. He was no stranger to jails. What worried him more was the fact that he wasn't going to be able to get to his horse and remove the $75,000 hidden in his saddle-bags. Culp had risked a lot for that money.

He'd worked hard for it. He'd already had to outrun some lawman they had put on his tail. Luckily Culp had lost the man somewhere down Yuma way. He'd been figuring himself pretty smart until now. Then he'd gone and let himself get hooked like some barefoot farmboy down from the hills. All because he'd gotten itchy pants over a redheaded saloon girl when she'd rolled her eyes and twitched her tight little ass!

As they reached the jail Duggan stepped ahead and shoved open the heavy door. Culp followed him inside. Behind him Koch closed the door with a solid thump.

'Customer, Phil,' Duggan said to the man behind the large, cluttered desk.

The man stood up. He was large, powerfully built, with a thick body. His stomach bulged tautly against his tan shirt. In the yellow lamplight his bald head gleamed, giving him a cold, impersonal appearance. He moved around the desk, staring intently at Culp, absently fingering the thick mustache which adorned his upper lip.

'What'd he do?' he asked shortly. His words were brittle, snapped out quickly. Culp judged him as a man who lived on his nerves.

'Would've raped Louella if we hadn't come along,' Duggan stated. 'Right, Koch?'

Koch leaned against the edge of the desk, nodding eagerly. His eyes glittered brightly.

'Damn right!'

'No it ain't!' Culp burst out. He knew he was

being foolish but he couldn't stop himself from speaking.

'He's got a loose mouth, Duggan,' the bald-headed man said. 'For Christ's sake close it!'

Culp knew what was coming and he tried to defend himself. But Duggan and Koch were old hands. They cornered Culp and dealt with him in a brutally methodical way that was far more frightening than the actual physical beating. When they were done they stepped back and appraised their handiwork with the air of true professionals.

Harry Culp lay in a haze of pain. His body pulsed with terrible intensity, as if every bone was broken, every organ ruptured. It hurt to breathe. It even hurt to think. When his eyes were able to focus again he stared at the scuffed floorboards and realized that the red spots he could see was his own blood. The bastards! What the hell had he walked into?

'Get him on his feet!'

Hands grabbed his clothing. Culp was hauled roughly to his feet and dragged over to the desk. He stared through badly swollen eyes at the bald-headed man, wishing silently that he had a gun in his hand.

'My name's Sherman,' the man said. 'This badge says I'm the law in Liberty. Long as you're in my jail you remember that. I got one rule. Do as you're told – every time. You just found out what happens if you don't!'

Culp stayed silent. He learned quickly. It was

one way of staying alive. In this place it looked like it was the only way of staying alive.

Sherman fingered his mustache. 'Nothing to say? Glad to see we understand each other.' He jerked a thick finger in Duggan's direction. 'Put him in a cell then get back in here so we can sort out the paperwork for the judge.'

Culp was dragged through a door and along a short passage. He received a distorted picture of bare stone walls, flickering lamps. The passage opened out on to the cell area. Culp was shoved into an empty cell. He lay on the cold stone floor and heard the door clang shut. The key rattled in the lock. Duggan and Koch vanished along the passage, leaving Harry Culp alone, hurt, and not just a little scared.

He didn't sit up for a long time. For some odd reason he had the impression he was being watched. He felt sure that the moment he moved Duggan and Koch would appear to start beating him again. The fear stayed with him for some while. He eventually dispelled it as nothing more than reaction. He was being stupid. Letting his imagination scare him. But he knew it wasn't imagination. He had come up against lawmen like Duggan and Koch before. Violent men who used their badges as an excuse for expressing their brutal characters. The other one, Sherman, was no different. Yet there was more to it than the initial violence. Culp couldn't put his finger on it but the feeling was there.

A chill ran through his aching body. Culp sat up, cringing against the cruel pain racking his tortured flesh. He stared around the cell. It was empty save for a low cot against the rear wall. He stumbled to his feet and went over to it. There was a thin mattress on the cot, with a crumpled blanket half hanging to the floor. Culp wrapped the blanket around him and lay down. After the discomfort of the stone floor the cot felt almost luxurious. Culp lay staring through the bars of his cell, watching the door at the far end of the short passage, wondering what was going on in the office.

Much later the door at the end of the passage opened and a figure stood in the doorway, a dark shape against the yellow light flooding out from the office. The figure remained in the doorway for some time, then retreated into the office. The door was firmly closed again. Harry Culp saw nothing. Sheer exhaustion had dragged him into a deep, restless sleep, and he didn't open his eyes until the cold light of dawn was pouring through the barred window of his cell.

He felt too stiff to move at first. The angry pain of the night before had become a dull, nagging ache. Culp's left eye was swollen horribly and his crushed lips began to bleed when he opened his mouth. When he tried to sit up the effort brought a groan of agony from him. Duggan and Koch had really worked him over! Jesus, he was going to be stiff for days!

The door at the far end of the passage crashed

open. Culp heard the sharp rap of footsteps on the stone floor. He lifted his head and saw Sherman staring at him through the bars of the cell.

'Nice day outside, boy,' Sherman remarked. 'Good day for a hanging, like they say!' He laughed sharply. 'Judge'll be here right quick.'

'Sheriff,' Culp called as Sherman turned away from the cell.

Sherman turned back to stare at him. 'You want something, boy?'

'You mind if I ask a question?'

'Go ahead.'

'Just what am I going to be charged with?'

Sherman tugged at his mustache. 'Thought you heard last night. Well, first there's the attempted rape of Louella Brill. Then you went and offered my two deputies a bribe, and when they wouldn't take it you assaulted them. Naturally they were forced to defend themselves and you sustained certain injuries.'

Culp shook his head in disbelief.

'Sheriff, you know and I know that's a pack of lies.'

'True, boy, but it's your word against mine and my deputies. I'll have to remind you that you did try to buy off my boys.'

'It was a shakedown,' Culp protested.

'Tell it to the judge.'

'You figure that'll do any good?' Culp asked drily.

Sherman shrugged. 'Never know your luck, boy.'

'In this town?' Culp laughed harshly. 'No chance, Sherman.'

'You should of thought about that before you stopped over.'

The deputy named Duggan appeared.

'Judge is here.'

Sherman nodded. 'Open him up.'

Duggan unlocked the cell. They led Culp into the office. The other deputy, Koch, was there. Sitting behind Sherman's desk was a silver-haired, lean man dressed in sombre black. He stared at Culp through glittering black eyes. The hands resting on the desk were long and thin, the pale skin translucent enough to show a fine tracery of veins.

'Read the charges against this man, Sheriff,' the seated man instructed. His voice was dry, emotionless.

'Deputies Duggan and Koch were forced to apprehend the prisoner in the act of sexually assaulting Miss Louella Brill. The prisoner then offered them money to forget what happened, and when Duggan and Koch refused this bribe he attacked them. His injuries are a result of their having to defend themselves.'

The judge glanced at Culp.

'Do you have anything to say in your defence, Culp?'

'Damn right I do! I don't know what kind of a town you crooks are running but don't expect me to just go quietly. This whole thing is rigged. All the way down the line from that little whore to this so-called trial.'

'Have you finished?' the judge enquired.

'For now,' Culp said. He had realized that he was wasting his breath. It made no difference what he said. It wasn't going to change a thing. Not a damn thing!

'Culp, in view of your aggressive attitude towards this court and its members, I feel no compunction towards reaching a liberal verdict. On the evidence presented to me in Sheriff Sherman's written report, plus the testimony of Miss Brill and the two deputies, all of whom I have spoken to at length, I find you guilty on all counts. I sentence you, therefore, to six months' hard labour. Sentence to commence immediately. This session of Liberty County Court is concluded. Remove the prisoner!'

2

Frank Angel took his horse easily up Liberty's main street, his gaze taking in the layout of the neat and tidy little town. It was the only way he could describe Liberty. It was a township which had sprung up in the first instance to serve the cattle community developing in the area. Over the years it had become established, more and more businesses opening up, a greater flow of families moving in. Gradually, though still supplying the outlying ranches, Liberty became independent. It prospered and took on an identity of its own. Unlike any ordinary cattle-town Liberty went further than was usual in its attempts to create a better image for itself. It showed in the clean streets, the cared-for, painted buildings, the atmosphere of orderliness pervading the quiet calm. For some reason he couldn't figure Frank Angel found Liberty just a little too good to be true. There was a feeling he had about the place, despite the fact he'd only just ridden in. Perhaps, he thought, it

15

was just his suspicious nature. He never had been one for taking things at face value. Angel always liked to look a little deeper. It was surprising what a glance behind the scenes often revealed. Idly he wondered what Liberty's skeleton in the cupboard looked like.

Angel reined in before a small establishment that advertised 'Good Food' and eased himself stiffly from the saddle. He looped the reins over the hitch rail, stepped up on to the boardwalk and went inside the restaurant. The interior reflected Liberty's overall appearance. The place was clean, bright, neatly arranged. The eight tables were all covered by fresh, blue-and-white-checked cloths. The aroma of frying steak, drifting through from the kitchen in the rear, indicated that the standard of cooking would be as high as that of the interior decoration. Satisfied that he was going to have a good meal, Angel sat down, choosing a table by the window, which also allowed him a clear view of the door. He hadn't been seated for more than a few seconds when he heard movement behind the counter and a girl with dark hair and green eyes appeared from the kitchen.

The hair and the eyes were the first things to catch Angel's attention. The hair because it was thick and long and shone like he'd never seen hair shine before. The eyes were beautiful, striking, a shade of intense, sparkling green. They were both sensuous and mischievous, a combination Angel found irresistible. His interest was further aroused when the girl crossed over to his table, smiling at him as though they were old and very good friends. She was wearing a plain, light-blue dress that did wonders for her long-legged, slim figure, and Angel found it wasn't doing him any harm.

'My first customer of the day,' the girl said pleasantly. 'I always make a rule to give the first customer the very best service.'

Angel couldn't help smiling. With a line like that she was bound to go far.

'I've ridden a long way since this morning,' he said, 'so I warn you I'm a hungry customer.'

'How about steak, with fried onions. Browned potatoes, greens, gravy. To follow I've got fresh apple-pie with cream that was still in the cow a few hours ago.'

'If you could bring me a pot of coffee to start it'll do just fine.'

The girl nodded and returned to the kitchen. Angel sat back and gazed out through the window. There weren't very many people out on the street. Liberty seemed to have retired for lunch. He wondered where Harry Culp was – if the man was still in Liberty. Angel had lost a lot of time due to getting himself set afoot back in Arizona. Then he'd gone and walked in on that business with the Reece brothers and the Apache raiding-party at that way station. Matters had become a little difficult for a time and Culp had ceased to be Angel's prime concern. But the interruption was over now and Angel had taken up the chase again.

17

As the Attorney General's last telegraph message had suggested, he had picked up Culp's cold trail quickly, allowing nothing to distract him. The Old Man had a knack of being able to convey his personal feelings even through the mechanical and impersonal limitations of the telegraph's printed words. Angel had been in no doubt as to the Attorney General's annoyance. The Attorney General did not like his investigators breaking off from an assignment, unless the circumstances were very exceptional. Angel was left with the distinct feeling that his reasons – a dead horse and the combination of outlaw gang and warring Apaches – lacked what the Attorney General considered to be a justifiable excuse.

On his return to Yuma Angel had rigged himself up with a fresh outfit and had then painstakingly gone through the motions of tracking Culp. It had taken him three days to cut the trail, winding its dusty way across the heat-seared Arizona badlands, gradually slipping off towards the north-east beyond Lake Havasu, across endless, empty miles. The three days had become five, then six. Angel had managed to gain a little knowledge about Culp at each place he stopped for food or water or somewhere to sleep for the night. Each tiny, desolate town, each isolated ranch, all furnished some information about the direction in which Culp appeared to be heading. Angel couldn't guess at Culp's ultimate destination, whether the man intended to meet anyone. Not that those items really mattered. All Frank Angel wanted was Harry Culp and the $75,000 he had with him. Culp was wanted for his part in a complicated swindle involving government officials dealing in Indian affairs, namely the sale of land belonging to tribes in the south-west. The swindle had been broken up after long months of painstaking undercover investigation by the Department of Justice. Angel had only been put on the case during the final weeks, after one of the department's investigators had been shot down and killed in Tucson. He had been able to assist in the capture of the men involved – except for one. That had been Harry Culp. And Angel intended to right that wrong as soon as he could.

The town of Liberty, basking in the shadow of the Colorado Plateau, a tiny spot of civilization in the middle of nowhere, was yet another stopover in Culp's seemingly endless ride. Angel was sure the man had taken time to rest here after the long journey up into the rocky escarpments of the plateau. Beyond lay the dry miles of the Painted Desert and the whole of the way ahead, curving west and east, became a maze of rocky canyons and gorges, a rising landscape of mountainous terrain. It was a wide, empty, savage country, and if Culp intended crossing it he would need to stock up on his supplies. . . .

'Coffee!'

Angel was dragged out of his reflections by the sound of the girl's voice. He nodded his thanks and watched her cross the floor on her way back to the kitchen. The smell of fresh coffee filled his nostrils and he eagerly filled the large china mug she had provided. The coffee was delicious. Angel downed half the pot over the next few minutes, slowly beginning to feel part-way human again. It was only now that he realized the grubby state he was in. He hadn't shaved for a couple of days, his clothes were dusty, sweat-stale. He decided that as soon as he had finished his meal he would do something about his appearance.

A few minutes later the girl reappeared. She was carrying a tray holding Angel's meal. She smiled at him as she came across the floor of the restaurant. Without warning the smile vanished from her face. Angel heard the door rattle open, glanced that way, and saw two men step inside. The first thing he noticed about them was the aggressive, intolerant way they behaved. Nor was he slow to spot the badges they wore pinned to their grubby, creased shirts. The one in the lead was big, a heavy, beefy man with large hands. He grinned wolfishly as he planted himself squarely in the girl's path.

'Smells good, Jess,' he said. 'That steak'll do right well.'

The girl's face flared with anger. She made to move round the huge bulk but the man stepped in front of her again.

'Oh, for heaven's sake, get out of my way.'

Duggan laughed. 'My, don't she get uppity! Now you ought to treat us nice, Jess, 'cause we're customers. Ain't that right, Koch?'

'Yeah! Could be we want to spend some money here. Don't cost a thing to be civil, Jess.'

'How about showing us some civility and letting the lady through with this customer's meal!'

The man called Duggan turned at the sound of the strange voice. He eyed the speaker, seeing a tall, rangy young man in the act of rising from his seat at one of the tables. Duggan saw the dusty range clothes, the tanned, high-boned face, and thought he was looking at some out-of-work cowhand passing through.

'Hey, Koch, you hear something speak?'

Koch made a great show of staring around the restaurant. Then he shook his head.

'Thought I did. Must have been imagining it.' He hesitated for an exaggerated moment, then added: 'Mind – I can smell something.'

Duggan grinned. 'You know, so can I. Now what is it?'

'Cowshit!' Koch stated. 'Yeah. That's it – cowshit!'

'I've had just about enough of you two,' the girl, Jess, said angrily. She placed the loaded tray on the nearest table and swung round on the two grinning deputies. 'It isn't enough that this town has to put up with you and our so-called sheriff! Now we have to suffer your filthy humour and stupidity! I think it best if you leave my premises right now. One privilege I still enjoy is being able to refuse to serve anyone I don't wish to. In your language,

Duggan, it means you don't get to eat in here. Now get out!'

Duggan's face darkened, his small eyes glittering dangerously.

'The hell you say! Ain't no damn female going to tell me where I go! An' I'll eat here . . . now. . . .' Duggan reached out to snatch the steak from the plate resting on the tray.

'No!' Jess yelled. In her rage she swung a hand wildly at Duggan. Her small fist jarred the steak from his fingers and it fell to the floor.

Duggan gave a grunt of annoyance.

'Look what you done . . . stupid bitch . . . time someone showed you the way. . . !' He lashed out with a huge hand, slapping Jess across the face, hurling her across the restaurant. Behind him Koch uttered a shrill laugh.

Neither of them noticed that Frank Angel had moved. Silently, with fluid ease, he slid away from his table, crossing the restaurant in long strides. He reached Duggan's side just as the big deputy was about to move towards the fallen girl. Angel's right hand, held rigid, chopped brutally across the side of Duggan's thick neck. It was a powerful blow, delivered with practised efficiency. It caught Duggan in precisely the right place to paralyse nerves, and the big man went down without a sound. As Koch became aware of Angel's presence he made a desperate grab for his holstered gun. Angel twisted round to face him, his right leg delivering a swift kick. The toe of his boot caught

Koch's gunhand, sending the gun flying from dead fingers. Koch howled in pain, but even in his agony he was aware enough to use his left hand to snatch free the slim-bladed knife he carried in his belt. He slashed wildly at Angel's weaving body, missed, tried to reverse his thrust. By then Angel was on him. He reached out and grabbed Koch's wrist, twisting brutally. The knife slipped from Koch's fingers. Before it had touched the floor Angel had smashed a hard fist into Koch's exposed stomach. The deputy began to choke, gasping for breath. Angel clubbed him across the back of his neck and Koch went face down on the hard floor. He stopped choking and lay very still and very quiet.

Angel disarmed both men. He placed their various weapons out of sight behind the counter. Then he went across to where Jess was standing, her face white with shock. She regarded him with those startling green eyes, not yet certain how to take him.

'Is breakfast always so energetic in here?' Angel asked lightly. 'I've heard of working up an appetite.'

Jess couldn't help smiling. 'I don't know who you are but I'm glad you were here.'

'Frank Angel's the name.'

The girl held out a slim hand. 'Jessica Blake. Though everyone calls me Jess.'

'You feeling all right?' Angel enquired.

Jess nodded. She touched her fingers to the sore spot on her face where Duggan had struck her.

'Probably have a black eye in the morning,' she

said ruefully. 'That man has a kick like a mule.'

'Appears to have the brains of one as well,' Angel remarked. 'Is this kind of thing normal in this town?'

'If you asked anyone else you would find they had suddenly been struck dumb.'

'Not something that bothers you?'

Jess smiled, eyes sparkling. 'I come from a long line of ancestors who believe in calling a spade a spade. There's been too much dirt swept under the carpet in Liberty. I've not been one of those doing the sweeping. Trouble is, nobody in this town wants to listen.'

'Try me,' Angel suggested.

She studied him intently, frowning slightly.

'Maybe I shouldn't. You could already be in more trouble than you realize. Perhaps you ought to get on your horse and leave before those two wake up. They won't leave it as things are. I'm not trying to scare you, Frank Angel, but Liberty isn't your problem. Why ask for trouble?'

Angel grinned at her. 'You let me worry about my troubles,' he said. 'Tell me about Liberty.'

Jess sat down. 'Something tells me there's more to you than a dirty shirt and a couple of days' growth of whiskers. Just who are you, Frank Angel?'

'Might be better if you didn't know.'

Jess wagged a finger at him, 'Oh, no,' she said. 'You don't get off so easy.'

'Let's just say I'm looking for someone.'

24

'Here in Liberty?'

'Could be.'

'Man or woman?'

'Man. Name of Harry Culp. Does it mean anything to you?'

Jess thought for a moment, then she shook her head.

'For a moment I had a feeling I knew the name. Now I'm not so sure. Let me think about it. Thing is I get a lot of people in here who are just passing through. They buy a meal, then leave. It isn`t often I get to know their names. How recently was this man in Liberty?'

'A week back near as I can figure,' Angel said.

'Do you think he's still here?'

Angel shrugged. 'I don't know. He came this way and I'm certain he must have stopped here. It might only have been for a while. If he did then someone in Liberty must have seen him.'

'Maybe one of the saloons,' Jess suggested. 'Wait. I *have* heard the name.'

'From whom?'

'I remember now. It was just a snatch of conversation I overheard. Between a couple of the girls who work over at Jinty's Palace. It's one of the big saloons. And it was about a week ago. The girls sometimes come in here for an early breakfast after they've been working late. I was clearing a table and I heard one of them say something about . . . what was it . . . yes, she said she'd earned fifty dollars of easy money thanks to that Culp feller.

That was all. The only reason I recall it is because the name was new to me. Liberty's small enough for everyone to know all the local names. There isn't anyone around here named Culp.'

'Do you remember the name of the girl doing the talking?' Angel asked.

'Louella Brill. You can't miss her. She has red hair – and I mean red – and she's extremely – how can I put it – well developed for her tender years.'

'Where could I find her?'

'Most probably in the saloon,' Jess told him. 'Be careful in that place. It has a reputation for being pretty rough. Jinty McCall is a very tough character. He employs some violent people to keep the peace over there. They're the kind who hit you first and ask questions later.'

'Sounds like a fun place.' Angel picked up his hat. 'Sorry about the meal. You mind if I call back later?'

Jess smiled warmly. 'You call any time you like, Even if I'm closed!'

Angel indicated the sprawled figures on the floor.

'You want me to move them?'

'No,' Jess told him. 'I want to be here when they wake up.'

'That might not be advisable.'

'They don't scare me.' Jess crossed to the counter and retrieved the weapons Angel had placed there. 'Just dump these somewhere when you get outside.'

Angel took the weapons.

'You get any problems, just yell,' he said.

She followed him to the door, watched him untie his horse and move off along the street.

'Hey, I hope you find what you're looking for,' she called after him.

Angel smiled to himself. He had a feeling that whatever he found in Liberty it was sure to mean nothing but trouble for him. And as usual he was right!

3

Jinty's Palace stood at the far end of town, a three-floored, garish wooden structure. It was saloon, gambling-parlour and hotel, all under one roof. Angel was able to hear the noise emitting from the place long before he reached it. He left his horse at the crowded hitching rail and headed for the door. On the boardwalk he paused, remembering that he was still carrying the weapons he had taken from the two deputies. He turned, stepped to the edge of the boardwalk and casually deposited the weapons in the horse-trough he'd spotted beside the hitching rail.

A sour blast of warm air enveloped Angel as he stepped inside the saloon. He stood for a long moment while his eyes and his senses adjusted to the subdued light and the heady atmosphere. The air was hazy with cigar smoke and reeked of beer and cheap whiskey. Over in a far corner an out-of-tune piano was struggling to make itself heard above the cacophonous din. The big main room was crowded and every man seemed to be talking, or laughing, or singing, or groaning, each according to his mood. There were women too, moving from table to table in their bright, skimpy dresses, pausing every so often for a word here, a smile, a teasing caress. Yet beneath the loose, friendly mask it was all hard business. The girls were there to sell drinks, or the thrill of the card-tables, even themselves if that was the customer's desire. They peddled their various wares easily, enticing with glib words, with persuasion, flattery. Whatever the customer wanted, he was promised the best, and the girls worked hard to prise him away from the bottles of cheap whiskey. If it was to the gambling-tables the unfortunate individual would soon be able to watch his bankroll dwindle to zero. He would be up against skilled gamblers, men who lived with a pack of cards in their nimble fingers. The suckers, who never were given a break, wouldn't even realize that they had been well and truly taken. The glassy-eyed, self-styled stud, on his way upstairs with some simpering, doe-eyed young girl, might figure he was getting more for his money than the poker-player, might just as well have saved his money. The girl, even as she was slipping out of her clothes, simulating heated passion and desire, would most probably be figuring out her percentage of the day's take. While she lay beneath his straining bulk, making out that she was half-way to paradise, her moans and cries urging him on, she would be smiling because she'd worked out that she could turn at least two more tricks before she completed her shift. And after she had overplayed her frenzied climax, waiting for her client to finish his own panting efforts, she would stare up at the ceiling, inspect the glossy sheen of her fingernails, or even make the momentous decision to have her hair done before she started work the next day.

All in all, Jinty's Palace, for all its pretensions, was nothing more than a come-on. An expensive, gaudy set-up. It was for the losers.

These were only superficial observations as far as Frank Angel was concerned. He was here on a different matter. He stood just inside the door, his eyes searching the crowd of faces before him. He wasn't interested in what Jinty's Palace had to offer. He was simply looking for someone.

A girl. A girl named Louella Brill. Someone who, it appeared, had been in contact with Harry Culp. And that contact might have resulted in some kind of communication. It didn't matter how slight. There might have been a word, a phrase spoken which might give Angel some indication as to Culp's destination. He knew that there was also the likelihood that Culp hadn't said a word to the girl. But until he asked her there was no way of knowing.

Angel caught sight of a young girl with bright-red hair. She was standing beside a table, nudging a balding, middle-aged man wearing the clothes of a cowman. The man, half-embarrassed by her attentions, was making a mess of trying to fill a glass of whiskey. The girl leaned over to whisper something to him, giving the other men at the table an unrestricted view of her full, ripe white breasts, straining against the thin bodice of her cheap, tight dress. Whatever she said to the man caused his hand to shake even more. Whiskey spilled on to the table top.

Threading his way through the crowd Angel approached the table. The girl, fast realizing that the elderly cowman wasn't going to respond to her performance, began to ease away from him. As her eyes drifted away from the cowman they came to rest on the tall figure of a young, travel-stained individual. The girl's smile returned. This one looked more hopeful, she thought. And a damn sight more interesting than the bald-headed old coot she'd just wasted five minutes on. She wet her full lips with the tip of her pink tongue and fluttered her long lashes.

'Louella?' the young man said. He had a soft drawl to his voice that brought a warm feeling alive in the pit of her stomach.

'How d'you know my name?' she asked.

Frank Angel smiled easily at the girl.

'Got it from a friend,' he said. 'Told me that when I rode through Liberty to look up Louella. Said it wouldn't be hard to find you. Said to look for the prettiest girl with the prettiest red hair a man was ever likely to see. So here I am.'

Louella sighed.

'I think you and me are going to be good

friends. How about buying me a drink on it?'

'Wasn't drinking I had on my mind,' Angel said. 'Can't we find somewhere a little more private?'

'Why sure, honey.' Louella pouted. She grabbed Angel's hand and began to lead him towards the stairs on the far side of the saloon. 'One thing I do admire is a man who knows what he wants and just goes out to get it!' She prattled on as they climbed the stairs, moving along the landing. Reaching the far end of the passage, Louella paused at a door. 'Well, here we are, honey.'

Angel pushed open the door and gestured for Louella to precede him. She waltzed ahead of him, swinging her rounded hips. Angel followed, closing the door quietly behind him. He watched Louella cross the small room and absently stroke her hand across the faded cover on the bed. She turned, a frown on her pale young face when she realized he hadn't moved from the door.

'Something wrong, honey?' she asked.

'No.' Angel glanced quickly around the room. A thin smile touched his lips as he spotted the heads of the nails that had been driven through the lower frame of the window, securing it firmly to the sill. A simple, but effective, precaution against a dissatisfied client skipping without paying for his pleasure.

Louella, with all the instincts of an alley-cat, sensed there was more to this situation than just a young cowboy seeking a quick roll under the sheets. She lost her smile very suddenly and the young face turned hard and cold.

'Hey, what's going on? Who the hell are you?'

Angel eased away from the door.

'Just someone who wants to ask you a couple of questions – honey!'

'Ain't no questions gettin' asked,' Louella snapped. 'Now you just get out of my way, 'cause I'm leavin'!'

'Just tell me where Harry Culp is, Louella,' Angel said, and watched her expression change. Before she spoke he knew Louella had met Culp – but she was about to deny it.

'Who the hell is Harry Culp? I never heard of him!'

'Harry's an old friend of mine,' Angel lied. 'I know you met him when he came to Liberty. All I want to know is where he got to.'

Louella's eyes flickered around the room. She wore a trapped, frightened expression. Watching her Angel realized that there was even more to this situation than he'd first thought. Just what had happened between Louella and Harry Culp?

'Louella, just tell me where Harry is and I'll be out of here before you know it.'

'Go to hell, you bastard!' Louella yelled. 'I don't know anybody called Harry Culp! Now, just let me alone! I got a job to do and you're wastin' my time!'

Angel took a step towards her. Louella took one look at him, then started to scream. She had a powerful pair of lungs to match her more than ample exterior dimensions. Her high, seemingly endless screaming filled the room. Angel shook his head sadly. There was little a man could do against a female in full voice. He knew too that anyone hearing the sound was going to assume the worst. If anyone came into the room he wasn't going to be given any chance at all to state his side of the argument. He placed himself in front of her, still shaking his head. His right fist came up in a swift, restrained arc. He clipped Loualla across the rounded tip of her chin. Her eyes glazed and she fell back across the bed. Silence descended.

Only for a few seconds. Angel heard a sudden pounding of footsteps in the passage. Matters were getting very rapidly out of hand, he decided.

He moved to the window and peered through the dusty glass. A few feet below the window he could see the sloping roof of an extension to the main building. Beyond that lay a dusty alley. Recalling what Jess had said about the men hired to keep the peace at Jinty's Palace, Angel figured it was going to be wiser to take the quick way out. He stepped back a couple of feet, hunched his shoulders, and went through the window head first. Above the shattering glass he heard the door crash open behind him, voices raised in anger. Then he was outside, dropping in a controlled roll on to the sloping roof. He let his momentum carry him forward: towards, then over the edge. As he fell clear he heard the solid crack of a shot. The bullet clipped the edge of the roof, splitting the weathered wood. The alley rushed up to meet him. Twisting his body Angel hit on his feet, absorbing the impact in another roll forward.

He came to his feet quickly, hugging the wall below the sloping roof as he cut off towards the street. He didn't hesitate but stepped on to the street and walked straight to where his horse stood at the hitching rail. Calmly he loosened the reins and led the horse away from the front of Jinty's Palace. He was working on the assumption that it was going to take a couple of minutes for the men up in Louella's room to got themselves organized and to follow him. They would probably decide against following him through the window and across the roof in case he happened to be waiting for them in the alley. So they would have to retrace their steps back through the saloon, making their way through the crowd of customers. And by that time. . . .

Angel walked his horse on by the restaurant. He would have liked to stop off for another talk with Jess but he didn't think the time was right. He needed to find a place where he could sit and think things out. He hadn't forgotten about the two deputies either. From what he'd seen of them and the way Jess had spoken of the local sheriff, Angel ruled out enlisting any kind of help from Liberty's law.

He found a dingy, run-down hotel up at the north end of town. It was close to the complex of cattle-pens that had been built during the early years of Liberty's existence. A toothless old Mexican waited with inborn patience while Angel unstrapped his gear and took his rifle. As Angel kicked dust from his boots on his way inside the old man led the horse away to the stable at the rear of the building. Wrinkling his nose at the stale air inside the stuffy lobby Angel banged his rifle butt against the scarred top of the desk. A listless figure levered itself from the shadows in back and shuffled into the dim light.

'You want a room?'

'They do tell me that's what these places are for,' Angel said.

The desk clerk sneered, the closest he could get to a smile, and fished a key off the board behind him.

'You stayin' long?'

'Maybe.'

'Two dollars a day.'

Angel paid for a couple of days.

'You let me know when that runs out,' he said.

The clerk nodded. 'Up the stairs. First door on the left.'

Inside the shabby room Angel dumped his belongings on the bed. He turned and locked the door. He crossed the room and spent a couple of minutes fighting the warped window, eventually getting it to open.

There was a washstand leaning against one dirt-streaked wall, with a chipped mirror hanging above it. The water in the big jug had a film of dust

36

on its surface. Angel poured some into the basin and rinsed his face. He peered at himself through the mirror, stroking his face. He turned to his saddle-bags and pulled out a rolled towel. Inside the towel was his razor and a cake of soap. He spent long minutes working up a lather with the cold water, then carefully shaved. When he'd finished he took off his dirty shirt and pulled on the remaining clean one from his saddle-bag. He unbuckled his gunbelt and draped it from the corner of the tarnished brass bedhead. Then he stretched his long frame out on the worn blankets.

Somewhere in this town was the answer to his question: what had happened to Harry Culp? Angel had established beyond doubt that Culp had stopped off in Liberty. He wasn't so certain now that the man had ridden on. If that was true then where was Harry Culp? And where was the $75,000 the man had been carrying with him? Had somebody found out about Culp's money? It could be a reason for his apparent disappearance. Men had vanished for a lot less than $75,000. Even killed for less. Angel didn't rule out the possibility. He decided to wait until it was dark and then make another try at getting Louella Brill to talk. He was sure she knew more than she was prepared to admit. He wanted to know what she'd done to earn the fifty dollars Jess had overheard her mention. Angel wanted another chance to talk to Jess too. There were things he wanted to find out about Liberty and its law.

He let himself relax. He had a few hours before nightfall. A chance to catch up on some of the sleep he'd missed over the past few nights. He couldn't go on for ever without some rest and now was as good a time as any. He didn't realize how tired he was. How much in need of sound sleep.

He didn't see the afternoon shadows lengthen. Nor was he aware of the softening light, the setting sun bathing the town in muted orange tones. He slept through the dusk as lamps were lit against the approaching darkness, and only stirred restlessly at some near-at-hand noise. At first it didn't register . . . and when it did he fought against the drug of sleep, clawing his way to consciousness . . . but he was too late.

They came at him out of the shadows, harsh whisperings reaching his ears. Angel lunged up off the bed, snatching for the Colt, but he didn't have a chance to reach it. Hard, brutal blows smashed at his body, caught his face. He was thrown back across the bed, stunned, wild with anger. He lashed out with booted feet, satisfaction surging hotly as he felt flesh connect with the hard leather. A man yelled obscenely. Hands caught hold of Angel, dragging him from the bed, He grunted in agony as a crippling blow took him in the stomach. He stumbled to the floor. Someone kicked him, pain flaring across his ribs. Now he could taste blood in his mouth. Christ, he thought, they're going to kill me! The thought flashed a warning across his mind, and he made to reach for one of the slim-bladed throwing knifes concealed in the tops of his boots. There was no chance. A great weight smashed down across his skull, driving him face down on the dirty floor, and he knew no more.

4

He woke to throbbing pain, his body reacting to the savage beating. He lay on the hard, cold floor of the shadowed cell, staring through the iron bars. At the far end of a short passage he could see lamplight showing beneath a closed door. At last Angel sat up, groaning against the brutal swell of pain. There was a dull ache over his ribs and the left side of his face felt swollen and pulpy. As his eyes adjusted to the gloom Angel found he could make out the shape of a low cot. He struggled to his feet and staggered across the cell. He lowered himself on to the cot, pulling the thin blanket around his body. He lay there and waited for something to happen. There was little else he could do. He'd taken a sound beating and it was going to be a few hours before he was recovered enough to handle any coming situation.

One way and another he seemed to have upset a few people in Liberty. He was curious to see what they might do next. Whoever they were. He was pretty certain that Liberty's law was involved. The why of it would explain itself in time.

Angel reached beneath the blanket, fingers searching the tops of his boots. A thin smile touched his bruised lips. At least they hadn't found his pair of knives. The slim, deadly Solingen steel blades, concealed in sheaths that had been incorporated in the linings of his boots, had pulled him out of trouble on more than one occasion. And there was always the thin wire garrotte secreted in a shallow groove in his leather belt. They were the tools of Angel's trade. If the need to use them ever arose he wouldn't hesitate. It was a lesson Angel had learned early: in a life or death situation there was no room for hesitation.

He slept lightly through the long night, waiting and watching, but no one came until the morning. Angel had seen the darkness evaporate, greying as pale fingers of sunlight trickled in through the barred window of the cell, edging slowly across the stone floor. In the cold, lonely pre-dawn hours Angel had slipped off the cot, moving silently back and forth across the floor, flexing and testing the bruised, stiffened sinews of his body. His muscles ached and it felt as if each joint was about to lock solid. But for fifteen long minutes he endured the discomfort, knowing that the difference between life or death could easily hang on how swiftly he could respond in a threatening situation.

Angel was back on the cot, motionless, when the door at the end of the passage crashed open, and the two deputies – Duggan and Koch – swaggered towards the cell. They peered in at Angel's still figure for a minute. Koch produced a key which he placed in the lock of the door. He released the door and swung it open. By this time Duggan had his gun in his hand. He stepped inside the cell.

'Seems a shame to wake him,' Koch said. 'He looks kind of cosy.'

Duggan apparently didn't share his partner's humour. He stepped to the end of the cot, caught hold of the end and tipped it sideways, spilling Angel to the floor.

'Cosy ain't what this son of a bitch is about to get,' Duggan snapped. 'If I had my way I'd stomp the bastard right through the cracks in this floor!'

Shrugging off the blanket Angel climbed to his feet. He stood waiting for Duggan's next move. The deputy's face reflected his inner hostility towards his prisoner, and Angel knew enough not to do any provoking.

'Forget it,' Koch said. 'The judge's waiting, and you know he don't like being delayed.'

Duggan growled something under his breath. He jerked his gun in Angel's direction.

'Out!' he said. 'And make it fast!'

They took Angel along the passage to the office. The sheriff was there and so was the man they called the judge. The judge was fiddling with some legal-looking papers. He glanced up as Angel was shoved through the door. Angel took one look at the judge's hard, lined face, the flinty eyes, and decided there and then that he didn't like the man.

'This the prisoner?' The judge's voice was as cold as the expression on his face. Sheriff Sherman nodded and the judge asked: 'He said anything?'

'No, your Honour,' Sherman replied. 'The prisoner has declined to give any kind of statement.'

'I don't like uncooperative prisoners,' remarked the judge. 'Seems to be a sign of non repentance.'

'Seems to me a man might be willing to repent if he knew what he'd done in the first place,' Angel observed.

The judge glanced up at the prisoner. His brow furrowed as he studied the face of the young man standing before him.

'I could almost believe you didn't know what it is you've done. You'll be telling the court you've lost your memory next.'

'Way the law treats a body in this town that's quite likely to happen,' Angel said.

Sherman smiled. 'Wish I had a dollar for every prisoner who's come in here with that old tale.'

'You figure I got these bruises playing the piano?' Angel turned to face the judge. 'Humour me, Judge, And tell me what I did.'

'First you savagely attacked two of this town's duly appointed law officers. You then made a nuisance of yourself over at the saloon known as Jinty's Palace, terrifying one of the employees before causing damage to the premises themselves.'

'I do all that?' Angel asked.

'Why did you come to Liberty?' The judge leaned forward to ensure he heard Angel's reply.

'Just looking for a friend. I heard he was here.'

The judge stroked his cheek.

'This friend – what's your business with him?'

'That's my affair, Judge.'

The judge slammed his hand down on the desk top.

'Smart-mouth me, my boy, and I won't let you forget it in a hurry! Now who is this so-called friend you say you came looking for?'

'I figure you already know that. And I don't think I'd be far wrong guessing it's why you're taking such an interest in me. Am I right or am I wrong – Judge?'

'I haven't an idea what you're talking about,' the judge snapped. He shuffled the papers on the desk before him. 'Sheriff, there isn't a name on these documents. Who is this man?'

Sherman's face reddened visibly. 'I . . . er . . . sorry, your Honour! You, what's your name?'

'Angel – Frank Angel!'

The judge hastily filled in the empty spaces.

'The prisoner is guilty on all charges. Sentence is six months' hard labour. Deputies, take him away!'

Sherman could hardly wait to round on the judge. He contained himself until Angel had been removed from the office.

'Jesus Christ, Amos, this is getting crazy! Why in

44

hell pull such a fool stunt with him? Damn it, Amos, he'll ask his questions at the camp!'

Judge Amos Cranford drew a black leather case from the inside of his coat. With careful deliberation he slid out a fine Havana cigar, which he had imported from Cuba, cut it and lit it. He gazed at Phil Sherman through a cloud of blue smoke and let a smile curl up the corners of his mouth.

'Of course this man, Angel, will ask his questions. It won't get him anywhere. When Duggan and Koch take him up to the camp they can have a word with Trench. He can pass the word to the prisoners that no one must talk to this man. You know how Trench runs the camp. Angel won't get so much as a hello.'

'I'm not so sure this is wise, Amos. Working the set-up on Culp was all right until we come across that money in his saddle-bags. Hell, there's a difference between screwing money out of the county for prisoners' upkeep and pocketing it and downright murder for seventy-five thousand dollars.'

'Phil, only you and I know about that money. Harry Culp is dead, so he won't be doing any talking. Your two deputies, Trench and his boys, they're involved in our other little scheme, so I don't figure any of them to go shouting their mouths off. I dare say that Trench will be willing to undertake staging another accident for us.'

Sherman's eyes widened with the alarm festered by Cranford's casual remark.

'You going to have Angel killed too?'

'The neatest way out, Phil.'

'Sure. Will we do the same with the next one who comes looking for Culp? And the next? How many do we have to get rid of?'

'Don't exaggerate the problem, Phil.' Cranford stood up and crossed over to stare out of the window. 'This man – Angel – is obviously a partner of the late Harry Culp. When Culp offered me a share of that seventy-five thousand to let him go, he hinted that it was money from some unlawful venture he'd been involved in. He was a fool! He was so ready to make a deal to get out of the camp and away from Trench that he forgot I already had the money and that he wasn't in any position to make bargains!'

'Yeah,' Sherman snapped. 'So Culp's dead and you aim to kill this Angel. Does that guarantee we'll be safe?'

'Got to take risks, Phil. Life'll pass you by if you don't have the nerve to grab the opportunity when it shows itself. God, Phil, it's a lot of money. More than the chicken-feed we've been making up to now!'

'You never complained before.'

Cranford smiled. 'True. But a man gets to a point where he wants to grow. He pushes his horizon further out and he needs to expand. Maybe you hadn't noticed, Phil, but there's a hell of a big world outside of Liberty.'

A scowl darkened Sherman's face. 'All I know,

Amos, is that even half of seventy-five thousand dollars isn't going to buy it for you!'

Cranford didn't reply to that. He gazed out of the window, an odd little smile flickering across his face. A half of $75,000 might not get me all I want, but the whole damn bundle sure will! The thought pleased him greatly, and he turned towards Sherman, beaming expansively. Don't worry, Phil, he thought again, you won't have to fret over the matter for much longer. That's one thing about being dead – all your worries die with you!

5

Angel squatted silently in the rear of the creaking flatbed wagon as it wound its dusty way up into the sun-blistered hills above Liberty. He wore heavy manacles on his wrists and legs, these being linked to an iron ring bolted to the floor of the wagon. Progress along the rutted trail was slow, the ride uneven, and Angel decided that he deserved every savage spasm of pain that ripped through his aching body. The fact that he was possibly on his way to finding out where Harry Culp was did little to soothe his mood of self-disgust. It was not hard for him to conjure up a picture of the Attorney General's reaction if he ever got to hear how one of his top investigators was conducting himself.

Koch was driving the wagon. Beside him sat Duggan, a sawn-off shotgun cradled in his arms, He appeared to be treating the whole trip as a huge joke – at Angel's expense.

'Like I said, Angel, you'll take to Trench's place.' Duggan grinned. He hitched himself round on the wagon seat. 'One thing about Trench – he just loves hard bastards like you! I swear I never met a feller enjoys his work so much as Trench!'

'Him an' that damn whip!' Koch giggled. 'I do reckon he takes that thing to bed with him!'

'I seen him lace a man's back open clear down to the bone!' Duggan stared at Angel's face as he spoke. There was no reaction and Duggan growled peevishly. 'Yeah, well, we'll see how tough you are when Trench gets his hands on you!'

'Is this where I'm supposed to say how scared I am?' Angel asked.

'Balls, Angel!' Dug sleeved sweat from his face. 'I don't reckon you're so damn tough.'

'I can live with that.'

Koch spat over the side of the wagon. 'Yeah, but how long for?'

The ride took almost four hours. Angel spent the time observing the silent, barren terrain they were passing through. A better place for a hard-labour camp would be difficult to find. Desolate, waterless country, where a man on foot would very quickly find himself in trouble. Survival would only be for the fittest. Any luckless individual who somehow managed to escape from the brutal privation of a hard-labour gang was likely to be less than fit right from the start. Angel wondered if anyone had ever escaped from the camp run by this man called Trench.

Or would he – Angel – be the first? Because that's just what he intended to do once he'd got the information he needed.

Angel willed himself to relax during the journey. He knew that in the time ahead he was going to need all his strength. There was no way of telling the kind of pressure he might be under at the camp. It was going to be a case of reacting to whatever cropped up – no matter what.

An hour after midday Koch swung the wagon over a steep rise and took it along the final stretch of the trail. Just below them, nestling at the base of a high, sheer rockface, lay the camp.

Angel's first impression was of an ugly sprawl of wooden buildings inside a wide, exposed compound. On three sides tall fences, strung with barbedwire, enclosed the compound. The fourth side of the compound was the sheer rockface itself.

'All the comforts of home,' Angel observed drily as Koch brought the wagon to a halt before the closed gates of the compound.

Duggan, in the act of stepping to the ground, threw him an angry scowl.

'Mister, in a couple of days you'll wish you'd never of left your mammy's side!'

Angel watched him trudge to the gates as they were opened by an armed guard.

'Ain't a funny bone in his whole body,' he told Koch.

Koch glanced back over his shoulder.

'You try that clever talk on Trench an' you won't have a bone that ain't broken! An' I ain't jokin'!'

As soon as the gates were open Koch rolled the wagon into the compound. With Duggan following on foot Koch took the wagon over to the largest of the wooden buildings.

'I'll go find Trench,' Duggan said and vanished inside.

Koch climbed down from the wagon. He strolled round to the rear, fishing a key from his shirt pocket.

'You get any ideas about running, Angel, just take a look round,' he warned as he unlocked the manacles securing Angel to the wagon floor.

Angel had already taken a good look round. His initial count had totalled six armed guards. He hadn't missed the wooden tower either, rising to about fifteen feet, and placed so that it gave anyone perched on the covered platform an unobstructed view over the whole compound. On the face of it the place appeared escape-proof. But Angel didn't believe in such theories. The compound had been created to imprison men, by men, and that led to the natural conclusion – it could be defeated by a man.

He leaned against the rear of the wagon, apparently unconcerned by his surroundings. Koch stood a few yards off, watching Angel intently.

'He the one?'

Angel glanced up at the new voice. The man standing beside Duggan had to be Trench. Tall and heavy-built, with a broad, loose-fleshed face, Trench gave off an air of brooding menace. He glared at Angel with fierce, strangely pale eyes.

'Duggan tells me you fancy yourself a hard bastard! That right, Angel?'

Angel didn't reply. He didn't figure to give Trench any excuse to use the whip looped around his thick waist.

'Aw, he's done gone and swallowed his tongue!' Duggan grinned.

'Trench'll shake it loose,' Koch said. 'What say, Trench?'

'We got ways'd make a wooden Injun talk,' Trench agreed. 'Now, you boys can go home, an' me an' Mister Angel can get acquainted.'

Duggan and Koch climbed back on to the wagon. Angel stepped aside as Koch turned it around.

'Pity we had to lose you so soon,' Duggan said as the wagon rolled on by Angel.

'Ease your mind, sonny,' Angel whispered. 'We'll be meeting up again 'fore long! I promise!'

The smile faded from Duggan's face, and then he was gone, the wagon rattling across the compound towards the gates.

'All right, Angel,' Trench said. 'Let's move! This ain't no old ladies home!'

Trench called over one of the armed guards and Angel was escorted across the compound. He was taken to one of the smaller huts. The interior was bare except for a row of wooden cots running the length of the narrow building. The air was hot, stale, reeking of sweat and urine.

'We try not to make our guests too comfortable,' Trench said. 'They don't spend too much time in here. Plenty of work for 'em building the new road over the mountain. Come dawn tomorrow that's where you'll be, Mister Angel!'

'Beats sitting around,' Angel smiled.

'Let's see how many jokes you tell after a day up on that pile of rock,' Trench said. He walked along the row of cots, stopping beside one. 'This one's vacant. Use it, Angel. Yeah, here's the way we run things. Only way in and out of this hut is by the door. Windows all barred. Floor's dirt and hard as rock. You don't come or go without instruction. Stop outside anytime day or night without getting the word and you'll get a bullet. And my boys have orders to shoot to kill. Just remember that and you'll stay alive. Don't matter to me one way or the other. It's your life. Understand?'

'It's clear,' Angel said. 'What does a man do when he wants to pee?'

'There's a bucket in the corner over there,' Trench said. 'Every man in the hut takes turns emptying it each morning.' He grinned at Angel. 'You got any complaints?'

'Working on a few.'

'After today, Angel, you ain't going to have much time to think about anything. So I'll leave you to it.'

The door thudded shut and Angel was left alone. He moved to one of the barred windows beside the door and watched Trench and the

53

guard making their way across the bleached, heat-hazed compound. He stayed by the window for a time, observing, silently calculating distances between buildings, how far from this point to that point, where the stables were. It was all information to be stored, held in reserve for possible use in the future. Eventually he moved back into the hut, sitting on the edge of his cot. Angel absently ran his hand over the lumpy, straw-filled mattress. It and the single, greasy blanket were filthy. Angel sighed. It wouldn't be the first time he'd shared his bed with a couple of thousand bugs!

He sat back and took stock of the situation. Apart from the fact that things had gone a little further than he might have intended, at least his appearance in Liberty, asking questions about Harry Culp, had created some ripples in somebody's dirty little pool! Angel was sure that Cranford, the judge, was in on it. So was Sheriff Sherman, and possibly the two deputies. Perhaps even Trench. All he needed now was proof of Harry Culp's stay here at the camp. A nagging little voice somewhere at the back of his mind was persisting in the notion that Harry Culp was most probably dead. Angel hated himself for allowing the thoughts, but the more he pondered on it, the stronger it grew. Harry Culp had ridden into Liberty with $75,000 in cold cash on him. Somewhere along the line he had fallen foul of Liberty's crooked law, probably in the form of a set-up, involving Louella Brill. That would explain the fifty dollars she'd earned.

It wouldn't have been the first time that a stranger to an isolated little town had found himself hauled before the local court on a cooked-up charge. The unfortunate victim, dazed by the sudden turn of events, would find himself charged and convicted and on his way to months of hard labour, long before he had time to say a word. The local citizens, who paid taxes for the upkeep of their county penal system, would figure they were getting good value for their money when they saw that the convicted felons were repaying their debt to society by building the new road the county needed so badly. Every prisoner in the care of the county had to be housed and fed, equipment required repair or replacement. That meant a size-able flow of cash.

If Angel's thoughts were moving along the right tracks, then a good proportion of that money was finding its way into the pockets of Judge Cranford and Sheriff Sherman. And that brought him right back to Harry Culp and the $75,000, and probably the reason why Angel had been so promptly removed from the scene. Somebody was sitting on all that money. That same person was likely to be hiding a murder too. Which added another dimension to Angel's position. If Culp was dead, the money concealed, the guilty parties weren't going to want too many witnesses walking around. Angel felt suddenly very expendable.

6

It was starting to get dark when the work-parties returned to the camp. Angel heard the rumble of the heavy wagons filling the compound. He stood by a window, staring through the bars, and watched the groups of weary, filthy prisoners being unloaded from the wagons by armed guards. As soon as every man had been accounted for the prisoners were ordered to their huts. Angel studied the group approaching the hut he was in. There were nine of them. By the time they reached the hut he had picked out the one who would have appointed himself boss. Angel knew that he would have to stand up to this man and beat him, if the need arose. Only then would he get what he wanted.

Angel was back on his cot when the door opened and the men crowded in, eager to get a look at the new man. The one Angel had judged as the leader of the group ordered the door closed.

He alone moved across the hut to stand at the foot of Angel's cot. Angel ignored him.

The man was as tall as Angel, powerfully built. He had dark, handsome features, marred by a thin scar running down his left cheek. His thin hair was black, curling at the nape of his neck. Large hands, with long, muscular fingers, flexed impatiently as he stared at Angel, silently demanding to be noticed.

'Hey!' he said at last, anger in his tone at having to attract attention in such a mundane way.

No response.

'You deaf, asshole?'

'No. And the name's Angel. But to you it'll be Mister Angel!' Somebody laughed. The man at the foot of Angel's cot glanced in the direction of the group of prisoners. The laugh froze. Silence returned.

'Well my name's Capucci, and I don't take any kind of crap from assholes like you!'

Angel smiled. 'There's a joke there somewhere, Capucci, but I'm damned if I'm going to explain it to you.' He stood up and placed himself directly in front of the man. 'Now the way I see it we all got trouble enough just being here. I don't need any more. But if you gotta prove you're some kind of big feller round here don't expect me to sit back and let it happen. I'll give you first try and then I'll put you down so hard your balls are going to drop right off!'

For a long moment Capucci stared at Angel, as

though he hadn't heard correctly. But then he realized that Angel had said what he'd heard, and being the man he was Capucci couldn't do anything other than react violently. He had already made his first mistake. He had allowed his feelings to show on his face. His eyes telegraphed his intentions, and Angel was already countering Capucci's punch before it had even reached any kind of momentum.

As Angel's left arm blocked Capucci's savage swing, batting the big fist harmlessly aside, his own right, sweeping up from hip-level, smashed across the side of Capucci's jaw. The sound of the blow came loud in the silent hut, the stunning impact throwing Capucci off balance, twisting him sideways. His legs caught the edge of one of the cots and he went down with a solid crash. Capucci's body arched once, lifting from the dirt floor in a spasm of agony, then he dropped and lay still.

Angel stepped over Capucci's motionless body. He strode across the hut to stand before the murmuring group of prisoners. Giving them a scathing glance he said:

'Who else wants to try? Come on, you sons of bitches! I'm just in the mood. Those bastards down in Liberty kicked enough shit out of me so's I'm good and mad. Well?'

Nobody spoke. Nobody moved. They all stared at Angel with enough resentment for the whole world. But that was as far as it went. Eventually one of them cleared his throat.

'Ain't any of us wants to tangle with you, mister. Capucci – he just naturally figures he has to show how tough he is.'

'How tough he was,' corrected a scrawny little man. He scuttled out from the group, eyeing Angel closely. His Adam's apple bobbed up and down in his thin neck. He reminded Angel of a damn vulture! 'Hey, Angel, what's so special about you?'

'I didn't know there was.' Angel watched the little man, trying to read what was reflected in the bright, beady eyes.

'Then why'd Trench warn us off talking to you?'

'He do that?' Angel was intrigued. 'Doesn't seem to have stopped you.'

'Hell, Angel, Trench may be hard but we don't scare all that easy. I been in pens so tough they make this place seem like home. Trench ain't no more than a big fart! He's all wind. Why, take that goddam whip away from him an' he'd be no diff'nt the rest of us.'

The little man led Angel away from the front of the hut. They paused beside the man's cot.

'What do they call you?' Angel asked.

The little man grinned, showing yellowed, crooked teeth in hard shrunken gums.

'Birdy,' he said and laughed shrilly.

'So what have you heard about me, Birdy?'

'Enough. I hear pretty good. Couple of the guards were talkin' and Birdy was listening. 'Pears

59

you're a special case. That was why Trench warned us off. Trouble is something like that just makes me curious.' Birdy glanced round to make sure nobody was hanging around. 'The way I heard. it, Angel, this place ain't about to be very healthy for you!'

'Is that the way it was for Harry Culp?' Angel asked, eyes fixed on Birdy's face. He knew he was taking a chance mentioning Culp's name but he figured it was worth the risk. Birdy swallowed so hard his Adam's apple almost vanished. For a fleeting second Angel thought he'd said too much. 'Come on, Birdy, tell me!'

'He never stood a chance,' Birdy murmured. 'He knew they wanted him dead. Jesus, Angel, the poor bastard just had no place to hide from them. He was only here for four days and then he was dead.' Birdy shook his head. 'Bastards said it was an accident! Accident my ass! They made him work on a real bad stretch of the road all on his own. An' then a damn rockslide comes down right on top of him! Everybody goes runnin' to see if they can help him but I stuck around, keeping out of sight. An' I saw that Trench coming down off the slope where the slide started. He couldn't see me but I saw him. Saw him drop an iron lever-bar in one of the wagons too. Then he goes on up to where they're trying to dig Culp out of the rock an' makes all the right noises.' Birdy fell silent.

'You told anybody else about this?' Angel asked.

Birdy threw him a bitter glance.

'You think I want to end up like Harry Culp? Listen, Angel, I was there when they dragged Culp out of that rockslide! Ain't a sight I want to see again. You ever seen a man after he's been squashed flat like a stepped-on bug? He just didn't look like a man any more. Angel, I don't know why they tossed you in here but it seems it must be something to do with Culp. I was you I wouldn't admit to being a friend of Harry Culp's. Hardly worth all the trouble it'll bring you.'

'Only thing that's troubling me, Birdy, is how I'm going to get out of this place,' Angel said.

Birdy grinned. 'Ain't ever been done yet, Angel. But I'll stake my life you're the man to do it.' He stroked his chin thoughtfully. 'You . . . er . . . wouldn't be needing a partner . . . Angel?'

'All depends, Birdy. I'll let you know.'

Angel eased away from the little man. Birdy glanced up, wondering why Angel had moved so suddenly. And then he saw.

Capucci was on his feet. Swaying slightly he was staring in Angel's direction with open hostility blazing in his eyes. An angry blotchy bruise had already begun to form on his cheek where Angel's fist had caught him. Capucci repeatedly touched his cheek, wincing at the discomfort it was causing him. He held Angel's stare for a time, then reluctantly backed off. He stalked along the row of cots until he reached his own, throwing himself across it.

'Now you got more problems, Angel,' Birdy whispered. 'Don't show him your back 'cause he'll find something to stick in it if you do!'

7

In the chill dawn light the guards began to rouse the camp. Bleary-eyed prisoners, stiff from uncomfortable hours on rigid wooden cots, stumbled from the huts. They stood shivering in the compound until a nod from the guards allowed them to cross to the cookhouse. Here on long wooden tables, steaming iron pots held the only meal the prisoners would get during the day. Armed with a tin plate, mug and spoon, each prisoner shuffled along the tables, receiving a ladle of soggy beans, a hunk of dark bread and a mug of bitter black coffee.

Eyeing his breakfast with less than rapturous enthusiasm, Angel wandered over to a nearby hut and squatted on his heels. He placed his mug of coffee on the ground beside him while he ate. The beans were tough, flavourless, and the bread was stale. But it was all he was liable to get for some time, so Angel ate.

Birdy appeared and joined Angel. He sat for a

while, busy with his meal. He ate with the deliberation of a man who knew what it was like to go hungry.

'I see another bean after I leave this place I'll go crazy,' he said as he put down his empty plate and picked up his mug of coffee.

Angel smiled thinly. 'What happens when we leave here, Birdy?'

Lifting a scrawny arm Birdy indicated the distant peaks.

'We go up there. 'Bout hour and a half ride. Then we make a road.' Birdy drained his coffee. 'Nice when life's simple, ain't it, Angel!'

At that moment the guards began to move across the compound. The breakfast period was over. The prisoners were herded into wagons, each with two armed guards and a driver. The gates were opened and the wagons rolled out of the camp.

The dusty trail, grinding its way up the mountain slopes, was a crude, dangerous track. On one side the rocky slopes rose above the wagons, on the other lay a long, almost sheer drop to the jagged mass of tumbled stone below.

Frank Angel shut himself off from the physical discomforts of the ride. His mind was concerned with only one line of thought. How to get himself free. Until he did get away from this place there was little he could do to conclude the business of Cranford and Sherman. Like it or not he had stumbled on a nasty little racket being operated by the so-called law of Liberty. It needed stamping out

64

before anyone else finished up like Harry Culp. It was typical of life's complexities to bring a man to a place on one pretext and then go and drop into his lap a whole mess of other problems. As far as Angel could see his whole life had been one continuous round of swapping one set of problems for another. Not that he had ever worried over it. At least it kept life from becoming dull.

He heard a sudden shout. The wagon lurched, slipping sideways. Angel glanced over the side and saw that the front wheel had gone clear off the edge of the trail. The driver was fighting the jittery horses and not doing too well. The wagon jerked forward a little, then slid back again. Loosened rocks and dirt cascaded over the edge of the trail, rattling down the long, shale slope. Glancing at the slope Angel realized that they had left the earlier sheer drop far behind. Now this steep, but comparatively easier slope lay below.

Angel took one look at the slope and saw instantly a chance for escape. A slim chance, with the odds stacked against its being successful, but none the less a chance. Angel had learned through bitter experience that in his line of business opportunities were there to be grabbed with both hands.

The guard, perched on the seat beside the driver of the wagon, hunched himself round, eyes wide with fright as he anticipated being hurled over the edge of the trail.

'Get out!' he yelled. 'Move, you bastards! Jump!'

The prisoners surged towards the far side of the wagon. Angel moved too – but he crossed to the opposite side. He didn't hesitate. In the scant seconds before he went over the side of the wagon he heard a familiar voice somewhere close.

'I'm with you, Angel!'

Out of the corner of his eye Angel caught sight of Birdy. The skinny little man, moving with surprising agility, was sticking to Angel like a second shadow.

Angel hurled himself over the side of the wagon, dropping towards the near-vertical slope. He struck the loose sale on his feet, falling forwards. He didn't try to hold himself back because there was no way he was going to be able to control his descent. Angel allowed his body to go slack. The downward fall seemed endless. The world spun about Angel as he was catapulted clown the slope. Dust billowed up around him, acrid, blinding dust. It stung his eyes, clogged his nostrils, filled his lungs. A roaring noise blotted out every other sound.

And then with startling abruptness it all stopped. Movement and sound ceased. Angel lay, stunned, almost paralysed. He couldn't have lain there for more than seconds but it had the feel of eternity. Dimly, sound and feeling returned. Far off Angel heard angry voices. He lifted his head, pawing gritty dust from his eyes. A single rifle shot sounded. The bullet whacked into the earth yards to one side of where Angel lay. He jerked to his feet hurriedly while the echo of the shot faded among the rocks. Throwing a swift glance up to where the abandoned wagon now hung half-way over the edge of the trail, Angel made out the tiny figures of the armed guards, some of them pushing curious prisoners back from the rim of the trail. Other guards began to put rifles to shoulders. Angel decided it was time to move. He turned, cutting across an open stretch of ground. Yards away thick brush offered scant shelter. Beyond lay broken stretches of crumbling, eroded rock.

'Angel!'

The whispered call came from Angel's right. Birdy's scrawny figure dragged itself out of a clump of thorny brush. He looked extremely sorry for himself.

'You're liable to get your ass shot off if you don't get moving,' Angel told him brusquely.

Birdy managed a wry grin as he fell in beside Angel.

'Hey, we got company, Angel! Did you know? Friend of yours!'

Angel followed Birdy's finger. Moving in their direction, obviously intending to conceal himself in the brush, was Capucci. He glowered in Angel's direction, seemingly offering to fight Angel if he even threatened to make any kind of objection.

'Capucci's a son of a bitch,' Birdy said conversationally, 'but he's a hard one. Trench ain't going to let us go easy, Angel. The way things might get we might end up being grateful Capucci's along!'

'We? I'm starting to get the feeling I've suddenly got more friends than I ever realized,' Angel grunted.

They reached the brush and plunged on through, ignoring the clawing bite of thorn tendrils clutching at flesh and clothing. The sporadic gunfire coming from the distant rise behind then was spur enough to keep them moving.

'Won't take 'em long to find a way down that hill,' Birdy yelled. 'They come after us they'll be shootin' first and sayin' sorry while they bury us!'

'Yeah?' Angel managed a tight grin. 'They do tell me you got to catch your bird before you pluck it.'

Capucci, who was close enough to hear Angel's words let go a derisive snort.

'Easy enough to talk – Mister Angel!'

Angel didn't reply. Even so he admitted that Capucci was right. Talk was easy enough. Backing up those casual words was where the difficulty arose.

The brush thinned out just before the first outcropping of rook. Angel led the way in amongst weathered stone already too hot to touch. The jumbled mass of stone contained the oppressive heat and it radiated up off the ground and from the curving walls of rock. It sucked the moisture from their overheated bodies, leaving them damp and sticky with sweat.

Angel called a halt. Each man selected himself a

place where he could sink down on his heels. For a time there was silence, broken only by their harsh breathing as tortured lungs fought to supply weary bodies with life-giving air.

'Shit, Angel, this is crazy!' Capucci suddenly exploded. 'What the hell we doin' sitting here like it was a Sunday picnic? Trench's boys ain't going to be standing around playing with themselves!'

Angel raised his head. Sweat glistened on his brown face, mingling with the grimed filth to give him a savage expression.

'Let's get something straight, Capucci. I didn't ask for company. Right now I'm in enough trouble to keep me going for a long time. The last thing I need is you round my neck. If you don't like the way I'm doing things, mister, all you have to do is leave!'

Capucci half-rose from his position, then paused, as if something had caused him to hesitate. Indecision clouded his face, then he resumed his former pose.

'Angel, hey, Angel,' Birdy said. 'Take us out of here, Angel. You can do it!'

8

Phil Sherman shouldered his way past Amos Cranford the moment the judge opened the door of his neat, white-painted house. Cranford closed the door and walked down the passage, entering the room he used as his office. He ignored Sherman while he closed the door, crossed the room and seated himself behind his desk. Leaning back in his large leather armchair Cranford surveyed the panting, sweating sheriff calmly.

'Something wrong, Phil?'

'You better believe it, Amos,' Sherman almost yelled. He pulled a crumpled sheet of buff paper from his hip pocket and waved it under Cranford's nose. 'I said things had gone too far. This time we went and hung ourselves!'

'Calm down, Phil, before you wet your goddam pants. Just tell me what it is that's got you excited.'

'I told you I was worried about that Angel feller. More I thought about him the worse it got. So I did some checking, Amos. Sent a couple of wires to people I know.' He shook the paper he was holding. 'I got this back from a feller I know works in the federal building in the capitol. He owed me a favour and by God he's paid me in spades! Frank Angel, the man you sent out to Trench's camp, the man you figure to have killed – he ain't no drifting hardcase, Amos! He's a special investigator for the Justice Department. Works out of Washington for the goddam Attorney General! Jesus Christ, Amos, we're way out of our depth this time!'

Cranford remained silent while he absorbed Sherman's news. He glanced across the desk, smiling inwardly as he studied Sherman's wet, flushed face. The man was coming apart, he thought. Sherman was close to absolute panic. Cranford realized that his earlier decision to get rid of Sherman had been the right one. The matter was even more urgent now. Sherman could split the whole damn affair wide open if he was left to his own devices. Scared the way he was Sherman might simply walk out and start talking to the first person willing to listen. Critical as the situation might appear, Cranford still considered it possible to come out on the winning side. But not with Sherman around.

'Well?' Sherman demanded. 'You just going to sit there and play games?'

'Just thinking ahead, Phil.' Cranford smiled. He stood up. 'Look, Phil, let's just take things easy. I don't think we have anything to worry about.'

'Is that supposed to make everything all right?

Because you figure we ain't got problems?'
Sherman laughed harshly. 'Let me give you the
news, Judge. We've got more trouble than you ever
saw. This time it ain't some saddletramp we framed
and tossed in jail. This time it isn't going to be so
easy to forget. Christ, Amos, this is the government
we're playing with. Angel's a federal agent!'
Sherman's voice began to rise. 'Anything happens
to him this town's going to be crawling with Justice
Department people. I seen those boys at work
once before an' they don't ever let go once they
got you tabbed!'

'Give me a chance to think this out, Phil,'
Cranford suggested. 'Don't worry. I'll work on
something. You go back to your office. Just carry
on like it was a normal day. Later tonight come
back. Take the back way. Fewer people know what
we're doing the better.'

'We'll have to be smart to get out of this, Amos,'
Sherman said, slightly calmer now that Cranford
seemed to be taking control of the situation.

'Leave it to me, Phil. I won't let you down. We're
not finished yet.' Cranford came around the desk.
He put an arm across Sherman's shoulders as he
guided the sheriff out of the room, towards the
front door. 'You leave this to me. I'll see us
through.'

Cranford closed the door after Sherman had
gone and leaned against the frame, his face set,
eyes cold, his thin lips drawn in a bloodless line.
Damn the man! Sherman was a stupid animal!

Ready to cut and run at the first sign of trouble. It always boiled down to the same thing. You could never trust people. Get involved and you had to depend on the strength of those around you. All it took was one weak link in the chain and everything was suddenly threatened. Cranford made his way back to his office. He sat down behind his desk, staring at the blank wall on the far side of the room.

First, see to it that Sherman was silenced. That was a matter to which Cranford would attend personally. After that it would be Angel's turn. And then. . . ? Cranford didn't plan any further ahead. He considered it better to take one step at a time. Once he had Sherman and Angel out of the picture he could sit back and decide on his next move. One thing he did know. Eventually he would leave this place. He'd come to hate Liberty. It was a dirty little town in the middle of nowhere and he'd had his fill. It had served his purpose over the last few years. His set-up, in partnership with Sherman, had brought in a steady flow of money. Nothing spectacular but it had built up slowly. The unexpected bonus of $75,000 from the man called Harry Culp had been like a gift from the gods. With that kind of money Amos Cranford could go far. And he intended doing so.

Throughout the rest of the day Cranford followed his usual routine. He took his midday walk to town and ate lunch. Later he visited a number of Liberty's businessmen, discussing various legal matters. Half-way through the afternoon he stopped off at the barbershop and had a trim and a shave. He only saw Phil Sherman once during the day. The sheriff was crossing the street as Cranford came out of a store. Sherman almost gave himself away but managed to control his jangled nerves and mutter a quick response to Cranford's hearty greeting.

It was a couple of minutes off five o'clock when a dust-lathered rider reined in before the judge's house. Cranford had returned only a while before. He spotted the rider through the parlour window and went quickly to open the front door. He had already recognized the rider as one of the guards from Trench's camp.

'What's wrong?' Cranford asked.

'We got trouble out at the camp,' the rider told him. 'On the way to the construction camp this morning three prisoners made a break.'

A sense of unease washed over Cranford. Even as he asked the next question he was certain of the answer.

'Who were they?'

'Feller called Birdy. Hardcase named Capucci. And the new one who came in yesterday. Angel!'

Cranford almost chuckled out loud. Of all the men at the camp Angel had to be the one to escape. You had to hand it to the man, Cranford thought. He was no fool.

'How's Trench handling it?'

'He's got the camp locked up tight. Every man

he can spare is out looking for those three.' The rider grinned through the dusty mask caking his face. 'Hell, Trench is even out himself! I reckon we'll get 'em 'fore they get far, Judge. They're on foot and they don't have a gun between the three of 'em!'

Cranford considered the facts and came to the conclusion that the lack of facilities weren't going to deter Angel. The man would improvize every step of the way and if the opportunity arose he would furnish himself with whatever he needed to complete his task.

Whether on foot or horseback, armed with a gun or his bare hands, the man named Angel would also stick rigidly to his predetermined line of travel, which would bring him ultimately to Liberty.

To that end, Cranford decided, he would have to prepare himself. One way or another, in the not too distant future, Liberty was going to have a rude awakening.

9

'I can't see what you're going to gain in Liberty,'
Birdy complained. He stared at Angel's tight-
lipped expression and knew he wasn't going to get
any kind of answer. The little man had learned
quickly in the short time he'd been with Angel that
if the younger man wasn't in a mind to discuss
something there was no future in pursuing the
subject. He grumbled darkly to himself, making
sure that his words were inaudible.

They were moving along a sandy slope. High
rockfaces soared jaggedly skywards all around
them. The terrain they were crossing seemed
endless. A tortured expanse of sun-bleached stone
and dust, grotesque cactus lurching starkly out of
the dry earth. Pale tendrils of dust followed in
their wake as they stumbled wearily across hard
earth, clambered over rocks that were so hot from
the sun that the briefest contact burned the flesh
of their hands.

For Birdy and Capucci the journey had become

a nightmare. Their suffering was made the more unbearable by Angel's complete indifference. He simply led the way without a word. Nothing appeared to worry him. His tireless, rangy physique seemed to absorb all that the elements threw at him. His long legs ate up the miles without pause.

'Hold it!' Angel rapped out, throwing up a hand for silence.

Capucci, stubborn to the last, rasped:

'I don't hear nothing!'

Angel said nothing. There was no need. Before any of them had a chance to do a thing, three riders burst into view over the crest of the slope just ahead of them. The riders and horses were streaked with dust and sweat. Every man carried a rifle, and as they spotted the three escapees they began to open fire.

'Scatter!' Angel yelled. He felt the vicious sting of a bullet burn its way across the muscle of his left arm. He turned and took long strides towards a scattering of rocks, moving in a zigzag pattern. Bullets whacked the hard earth around him. Angel blessed the fact that there weren't many men who could score a hit on a moving target from the back of a horse. Yet there was always the lucky shot finding its mark. Angel took a long dive groundwards. He let his body roll, paying no head to the bruising it was receiving. As he wriggled in amongst the rocks he heard the solid thwack of bullets gouging the protective stone. He curled up at the base of a high boulder, reached down and slid out one of his throwing-knives. Those bastards out there were looking for blood! Well they could have some, but it damn well wasn't going to be Frank Angel's!

He caught sight of a large shadow flitting across the rocks to one side of where he was crouching. Angel watched the shadows grow larger as the rider pushed his horse deeper into the rocks. He waited, estimating the distance he was going to have to send his knife. Slowly Angel rose to his feet as the horse's head appeared. His arm eased back in the final seconds before the rider showed himself. The rider's head was already turning in Angel's direction, eyes flickering in recognition. The man tried desperately to bring his rifle over from the far side of his body. By then Angel had already cast the knife. It winked coldly in the bright sunlight as it flashed across the empty space between Angel and his target. The rider uttered a shallow cry as the hard steel bit into the muscle of his neck. He let go of his rifle and tried to drag the offending blade from his body. Blood streamed from the wound, staining his fingers, soaking his shirt. As Angel approached the rider the man turned to stare at him with eyes already glazing over. A frothy burst of blood erupted from his loose mouth. Keeling over, the man toppled from his saddle. Angel grabbed the loose reins of the skittish horse and moved to tie it to a knob of rock close by. When he returned to pick up the fallen rifle the man was dead. Angel retrieved his knife and put it away. He unstrapped the man's gunbelt, put it on and checked the heavy revolver. For a second Angel gazed at the dead man, regret clouding his features for an instant.

Leaving the horse, Angel moved to the edge of the rocks. The other riders were still in sight, firing at a mass of rocks. They weren't making any attempt at talking Birdy or Capucci out. It seemed that Trench kept his word. He'd told Angel back at the camp that anyone breaking the rules could expect to be shot. Angel cocked the rifle. At least the rules were easy to understand. He put the rifle to his shoulder and shot the closest of the riders out of the saddle. The man hit the ground hard, cursing loudly and obscenely. Angel had put a bullet through his shoulder. The man rolled about on the ground, blood spurting from the wound, The third rider yanked his horse about, searching for the source of the shot. He spurred his horse forward, moving towards Angel, as if he was immune to bullets. Angel levered another round into the chamber.

'You hold that horse right there, friend!" Angel warned. 'I can take you out easy from where I am!'

The rider cleared his throat and spat into the dust. He leaned forward, peering in the direction of Angel's cover.

'Come on out of there, boy,' he yelled. 'Bad enough you tried to break out. Now you gone and shot one of us! Boy, you are dead already! Now get yourself out here and fast, you son of a bitch!'

'Hey,' Angel called, 'you understand Spanish?'

'What?' The rider scowled. 'Naw, I don't understand Spanish. Why?'

'I figured you might seeing as you can't understand English. I asked you to stay put else you're liable to got shot!'

'Balls!' the rider roared. 'Damn you, mister, I done wastin' my time!' Without another word he began to dismount.

Angel shot his left leg from under him. The man last control and fell face down on the ground. He yelled in pain and anger. Before he could make any kind of recovery Angel had stepped out from the rocks, crossed over to where he lay, and had kicked the man's rifle out of his reach. The man grunted bitterly, staring up at Angel.

'You bastard!'

'Shut your mouth,' Angel told him. 'Figure yourself lucky you ain't dead!'

The man began to reply, then thought about what Angel had told him and fell silent. He made no protest as Angel took his gunbelt.

Birdy and Capucci were coming across the clearing to where Angel stood. Capucci was carrying the weapons belonging to the man Angel had shot in the shoulder. He was also leading the man's horse.

'How the hell did you manage it?' Birdy asked. He took the weapons Angel handed him.

'I live right,' Angel told him. He returned to the rocks and brought out the horse he'd left there.

'Where to now?' Birdy asked. 'Angel?'

80

'You know where I'm going,' Angel said. 'Use that horse, Birdy. Go where the hell you like.'

'That's about the the only place you're going, Angel!' Capucci's voice rapped out the words.

Angel turned slowly. He watched Capucci step into the open, his right hand held close to the butt of the gun now strapped around his waist.

'Now what's eating you, Capucci?' Angel asked.

'I aim to kill you before I ride out, Angel,' Capucci stated.

Angel's face remained impassive.

'Why? Because I put you down?'

'Yeah! I didn't like that. I don't let no man just walk into my life and do that! So we settle, Angel! Here – now!'

Birdy threw up his hands in despair.

'Capucci, for God's sake! You must be crazy! You don't figure to kill a man just because he punched you on the jaw and knocked you down! Hell, Trench and his boys are swarming all over these damn hills, liable to show up any minute and you want to play gunfighters! What you got inside that thick head of yours? Horseshit?'

'Stay out of this, you little asshole!' Capucci warned. 'Put your nose in and I'll shoot it off!'

'That before or after you've buried me?' Angel asked.

'I don't like your funny mouth, Angel.'

'Capucci, I don't want to fight you. But I'm not going to back off and give you a chance to gun me when I ain't looking. I reckon you're a fool to push

81

this just for the sake of stupid pride but that's your problem.'

'Angel, I'm going to kill you! I'm going to blow you wide open, you smart-assed bastard!'

Capucci was grinning. A confident expression filtered across his face. His right hand began its swift movement towards the butt of the gun holstered on his hip. Capucci felt the tips of his fingers stroke the smooth wood, begin to curl around the shaped butt. He was watching Angel and Angel hadn't even moved. Capucci's eyes narrowed. Disbelief clouded his face. Angel hadn't moved – yet there was a gun in his hand. He hadn't moved . . . had he? Damnit, he hadn't! Capucci snatched at his own gun, felt the comforting weight as it came free from its holster. His thumb dogged back the hammer, his finger applying pressure to the trigger. He heard the whipcrack snap of a shot. A solid blow struck his right shoulder. Capucci felt himself turned about. He plunged forward, gasping at the white-hot pain engulfing his shoulder. The hard earth rushed up to meet him and he struck it with stunning force. The heavy gun slipped from dead fingers. Capucci lay in shocked silence. He twisted his head and stared at the glistening red mess of his shoulder.

Angel put away his gun. He glanced at Birdy, who was staring at him in utter silence.

'What was I supposed to do? Kill him?' Angel asked.

Birdy shook himself, blinking as if coming out of

a deep sleep. He watched Angel kneel beside Capucci and expertly fashion a bandage from a couple of strips torn from Capucci's own shirt.

'Capucci, you get on that horse and you ride, mister. Make sure you don't ride in my direction. Next time I see you I'll finish what you started here. Find yourself a doctor when you can. Please yourself about that. I don't give a damn.'

Angel stood up and walked to his horse. He swung into the saddle, turning to stare down at Birdy. 'I'm heading for Liberty. Ride along if you want. But I got business there that isn't about to win me any popularity contests.'

Birdy mounted his horse and fell in alongside.

'I'll ride a ways with you, Angel. I need the time to figure you out.'

They cut away from the place, swinging in a wide loop that would bring them in towards Liberty from the east. Angel was hoping to avoid further contact with Trench and his hired guns. He wasn't too optimistic.

Ahead of then lay an undulating fall of land. A criss-cross landscape of small canyons and ravines, jagged fissures striking deep into the rocky terrain. And hanging over it all the swollen orb of the sun, radiating sullen heat that flowed into every crack, every hollow.

Angel rode with his rifle laid across his thighs, eyes constantly searching for any sign of pursuit, any movement, however slight, that might reveal some concealed marksman. Trench's men had showed him the way they operated, and as far as Angel was concerned he would deal them the same hand. In a situation like this there was no time for the niceties of life. You were either quick or very dead!

'Angel, behind us!' Birdy's tone was urgent.

Angel reined in and swivelled round in his saddle, shading his eyes against the savage glare of the high sun. On a distant ridge, maybe a half-mile back, he could see five riders outlined against the brassy sky.

'Damn!' Angel watched the riders for a minute. 'Bet you those sons of bitches are sitting watching us right now, Birdy.' He gazed round, seeing nothing to offer him any kind of comfort. 'Well, they sure got us spotted now. All they got to do is keep coming.'

'Ain't much chance of losing 'em in this country,' Birdy observed. 'Between here and Liberty it's all the same.' The little man screwed up his face. 'Caught between a rock and hard place, Angel,' he said, using a well-worn phrase.

Angel smiled. He could have used that phrase as his personal motto. He'd been in the position so many times he took it for granted now as part of his life.

'Birdy, you picked a bad time to take a ride with me.'

The skinny man's shoulders lifted in a quick shrug.

'What the hell, Angel,' he said, 'where else did I

have to go? Least I'm out of that damn place. Worth it just for that.'

'You could end up dead,' Angel said as they rode on.

'We all end up dead sooner or later.' Birdy fell silent for a time. After a bit, unable to restrain his curiosity any longer, he asked:

'Tell me Angel, just who the hell are you? I got to know 'cause it's drivin' me crazy!'

Angel didn't reply. Instead he reached down to work something out of a slit pocket in his leather belt, something that caught the sun on its silver face. Silently Angel handed a circular badge to Birdy, watching the amazed expression cross the man's face. Birdy studied the badge closely, reading the words inscribed around the edge of the disc. Department of Justice, United States of America, it read, and embossed in the centre of the badge was the symbolic screaming eagle. Gradually a smile etched itself across Birdy's face. The smile widened and became a chuckle, which in turn rose until Birdy was laughing out loud.

'Jesus Christ, Angel, you sure fooled us all! And me – breaking out of jail alongside a goddamn lawman! Hey, if this ever gets out I'll never live it down!' The thought triggered off another bout of laughter. 'Wish I could've soon Capucci's face if he'd found out! One thing he hates is a badge-toter!'

Angel retrieved his badge and returned it to its

resting-place. He let Birdy calm down before he asked:

'How do you feel about the law?'

Birdy sighed. 'Hell, Angel, we all got a living to earn. Me, I been riding the owlhoot trail most of my life. Never did amount to much. Always small-time stuff. Just enough to keep me going. That was when I weren't in jail. I got this thing about being caught all the time. Just keeps happening. And I never been one for using a gun so I end up behind bars.' Birdy's face hardened. 'Mind you, this Liberty deal got me mad as hell. Wouldn't mind if I'd done anything.' He grinned again. 'Hey, Angel, truth is I was framed! No foolin'!'

'I know the feeling, Birdy.'

'You mean to tell me they took you, Angel? I thought you Justice Department boys were smart!'

'Yeah, that's what they keep telling me.' Angel smiled.

'Do they know who you are?'

Angel shook his head.

'Far as they know I'm just another stranger who rode in. I said I was looking for Harry Culp. Told them I was a friend.'

'But you ain't?'

'Culp was on the run. He was carrying seventy-five thousand dollars with him. Proceeds of the swindle he'd been involved in. I trailed him as far as Liberty, then walked in on the neat little set-up Judge Cranford and Sheriff Sherman have going.'

'So now you got to go back to Liberty and take 'em?'

'Something like that,' Angel admitted. 'Only I don't expect it to be the year's most peaceful event. Culp's dead. Murdered. They'll know I've found that out and I don't expect any of them to fancy ending up at the end of a rope.' Angel paused. 'You still want to ride with me, Birdy?'

'Could be interesting.'

'Birdy, I think you could be right.'

10

Late afternoon. The setting sun cast long, black shadows across the naked land. The searing heat of midday had slowly evaporated. Now a pulsing warmth flowed out across the earth.

Frank Angel and Birdy crouched in the shadow of a low hill and studied the town of Liberty. There didn't appear to be anything out of place. Nothing to suggest anyone waiting for them. But Angel knew different. There was nothing tangible. Nothing he could put his finger on. Just a gut feeling. An instinct. And Angel had learned to trust his feelings.

He knew damn well that by now Cranford and Sherman would have got the word he was free. That he had escaped. Trench would have sent word. Acting on the information Cranford would have arranged for a reception party.

'Looks pretty peaceful,' Birdy murmured. 'But they wouldn't want it to look anything except peaceful.'

'They know we're coming,' Angel said. 'They'll be waiting.'

'Ain't going to make it easy, Angel.'

'It never is easy,' Angel told him.

Leading the horses, they walked the last stretch. Angel approached the town in a wide circle, bringing them in at the rear of the buildings along the main street.

'We'll leave the horses here,' he said.

Birdy nodded and they tethered the animals in the shade of thick brush.

'Ain't going to be time to change your mind once we get in there,' Angel reminded Birdy. 'You still want to get yourself involved?'

'Can't be any worse than me trying to run on my own, Angel. Hell, man, I told you I ain't no gunfighter. I get out there with Trench's men chasin' me I'd be back in that camp 'fore you could whistle Dixie! That was if they didn't shoot me first. You saw the way those three were we tangled with.' Birdy grinned. 'I'll take my chance with you, Angel.'

'All right, Birdy. I'll tell you something so listen good 'cause I ain't going to say it again. If we come up against any of Cranford's boys remember one thing. If it comes to a fight I don't bother with rules. Any man who tries to kill me better be damn good and do it the first time. He won't get a second chance.'

Moving from cover to cover, utilizing every clump of brush, every rock, every rise and hollow

in the ground, Angel and Birdy closed in on
Liberty. Soon they were in a position to be able to
see clearly the trash-littered backlots of the buildings. Angel was looking for one building in partic-
ular. Once he had it spotted he led the way along
the fringe of brush skirting the very edge of town.

'That the place?' Birdy whispered.

Angel nodded. He crouched down and studied
the rear of Jessica Blake's restaurant. He could see
that a lamp had been lit in the kitchen against the
fast-approaching darkness and he could make out
a faint shape moving back and forth behind the
curtained window.

They stayed where they were for a good quarter
of an hour, until Angel had satisfied himself there
were no waiting gunmen in the vicinity. Convinced
at last that it was safe, Angel touched Birdy's shoulder and they broke out of cover, heading directly
for the rear of the restaurant. Angel tried the rear
door and found it unlocked. He eased it open and
stepped silently into the kitchen, Birdy close
behind him.

'Hello, Jess,' he said gently.

The slim figure, bent over a long table, tensed.
Dark hair swirled away from her face as she turned,
green eyes wide with surprise. The shock lasted
only a second.

'Do you think you'll be able to stop long enough
to finish your meal this time?' Jess asked.

Angel grinned. 'I wouldn't count on, it.'

'I heard what had happened to you. How did

90

you get away from that camp?'

'Saw a chance and took it,' Angel said.

'Did you find your friend?' Jess asked, glancing at Birdy.

'I found out what happened to him. This is Birdy. He was at the camp. He was there when they killed Harry Culp.'

'You mean he's dead? Oh my!' Jess shook her head. 'Can't you go to the law?'

Birdy grinned. 'Don't she know?'

'My last visit was too short,' Angel replied. He fished out his badge and showed it to Jess.

'So you weren't looking for Harry Culp because he was a friend?'

'No,' Angel admitted. 'Jess, don't take offence because I didn't tell you who I was. It's surprising how reluctant people become once they know I'm a lawman. One minute they're ready to tell you everything, the next, when they see a badge, they dry up. And it could have got you hurt if Cranford's boys had found out you'd been talking to a lawman.'

Jess reached out to touch his arm.

'Thank you for thinking of that. Do you think Cranford has found out who you are?'

'It's possible. He'll know soon enough when I tell him myself.'

'Is that why you came back to Liberty?' Jess frowned suddenly. 'You don't intend taking on the whole lot of them yourself, do you?'

'What I'd like to do is get a message to my boss

in Washington. Let him know what I've walked into here. Then if something happens to me there'll be somebody else able to deal with Cranford and his bunch.'

'I know Cranford, Frank,' Jess said. 'He's a hard man. I don't think he'd hesitate to kill you if you got in his way.'

'They already tried once,' Birdy said.

Angel quickly outlined the incident with the three guards from the camp. As she listened Jess moved to sit down on a wooden kitchen chair.

'You'll have to go slowly,' she said. 'I can't keep up with it all.'

'Don't try,' Angel said. 'Listen, Jess, is there a telegaph office in town?'

'Yes.'

'First things first,' Angel said. 'Have you opened up yet?'

Jess shook her head. 'I'm not due to open for another hour.'

'Birdy, I want you to stay here. I'm going to try for the telegraph office.'

'And then?' Jess asked.

'See if Cranford will listen to reason. Try and make him give himself up.'

'Wonderful, isn't it!' Birdy said.

'What?' asked Angel.

'Faith in human nature.'

'Birdy, I said I was going to ask him. I didn't say anything about him actually agreeing.'

Jess led the way through the empty restaurant.

At the window she pointed out the telegraph office. It was across the street, some fifty yards down. Not far under normal circumstances, Angel thought, but when you were possibly walking under the threat of a bullet it seemed an awful long way. He checked the rifle he was carrying. The revolver as well.

'Be careful,' Jess whispered as he eased open the door.

'My middle name.' Angel smiled.

He paused on the boardwalk, allowing his eyes to adjust to the gloom. That was one thing in his favour, he thought. The darkness. Though it was double-edged. It made it hard for his enemies to see him, but it also worked the other way round.

Angel walked slowly along the boardwalk, his eyes searching every pool of shadow, every doorway. He scanned the mouths of alleys, each darkened window. He stopped when he reached the spot that placed him directly opposite the telegraph office. Lamplight glowed in the small window of the squat, single-storey building. Angel stepped down on to the street and strode across. At the far end of the street he heard the unhurried step of a horse. He flicked his gaze in that direction, saw a rider dismounting outside a saloon. The man tied his horse and went inside. Angel sighed. He was getting jumpy. He was also becoming, slowly but surely, very angry. Angry at what had been done to him since coming to Liberty. He'd been framed, beaten up, tossed in jail, sentenced to hard labour. It was a pretty long list to say he'd hardly had time to take off his hat in Liberty. On top of all that he'd had to risk his life in escaping and been forced to kill to stay alive.

And it wasn't over yet. Not by a long way!

He hesitated before going inside the telegraph office. He was putting himself in Cranford's position. Assuming that the judge had found out Angel's true identity, he was going to do his best to have Angel disposed of quickly. One thing the crooked judge would not want was for Angel's superiors to hear what had been going on in Liberty. One of the ways they might hear was by telegraph. And that could mean Cranford's men inside the office. Angel slipped into the alley beside the building. He made a quick circuit, finding no other windows or door. The only way in or out was through the front. He returned to the front and took a quick glance in through the window.

The telegraph operator was seated behind his counter, bent over his machine. Lounging against the wall near the counter was a hard-eyed, heavy man who had hired gun written all over him. A second man sat hunched over a tattered magazine, facing the door.

Angel moved to the door, eased the knob, and pushed the door open wide. As the door swung open Angel stepped back out of sight, pressing himself against the front of the telegraph office. He waited. Not for long. He heard the sound of a chair scraping on the wooden floor, then the slow tread of someone approaching the open doorway.

'Probably some kids playin' about, Sam,' came a voice from inside.

'Yeah?' Sam snapped back. 'Then how come you ain't goin' to look?'

'You're nearest, old buddy!'

Sam made a low sound at the back of his throat. He eased his uncertainty by drawing his gun.

Angel watched Sam's approaching shadow loom larger and larger. He let the gunman reach the doorway. Sam peered out into the darkness. He saw nothing at first. The moment he actually did spot something it was far too late. The solid butt of Angel's rifle came round hard and caught him across the side of the face. Sam grunted and flew back inside the office. His legs ceased to function correctly and he stumbled to his knees. Angel was right behind him. He clouted Sam again, this time behind the ear. Sam went down without a sound. As the unconscious gunman hit the floor Angel booted the door shut, swinging his rifle round to cover the second gunman. The man was half-way through a hurried draw and he abandoned the idea when he saw Angel's rifle aimed at his stomach.

'Put the gun on the floor,' Angel said. 'Now kick it over here.'

Angel picked up the gun and stuck it in his belt. He did the same with the weapon belonging to the man called Sam.

'Now, friend, you lie down on the floor,' Angel told the gunman. 'Face down. Arms and legs spread apart. And you so much as breathe heavy, mister, it'll be the day they bury you!'

The gunman did as he was told, recognizing the harsh, deliberation in Angel's voice.

'You ready to send?' Angel asked the telegrapher.

The middle-aged man behind the counter nodded. Sweat glistened on his white face and he tugged nervously at his tight shirt-collar.

'I want you to clear the lines through to Washington,' Angel instructed him. He pulled a message-pad to him, picked up a pencil and began to write.

'Washington?' the telegrapher asked.

'Yeah. It's that place where the President has his office,' Angel said. 'Get those lines clear. Priority clearance. You know the drill. Now get to it!'

'Yessir!' the telegrapher said. He turned to his key and began to tap out his message. 'It'll take time,' he apologized.

Angel finished writing and shoved the message-pad across the counter.

'Just do it. Then send this message.'

The telegrapher completed his first message. While he waited for the clearance he picked up the message-pad and read what Angel had put down. His eyes rounded, showing the whites, and he peered over the rim of the paper at Angel.

'This genuine?'

'You figure I'm doing this for fun!'

The telegrapher smiled weakly and turned back to his key. The clearance came through ten minutes later and Angel's message began its long journey across those endless miles, all the way to the rambling old building on Washington's Pennsylvania Avenue. There would be an even longer wait for the reply. But it was something Angel had to receive before he left the office. He had to know that the Attorney General had read his report on the activities in Liberty. All Angel wanted was an acknowledgement.

It took almost an hour. Angel was beginning to sweat. The longer he remained in the telegraph office the more likely one or more of Cranford's men might walk in on him.

In fact that was what more or less happened.

Angel spotted three figures coming across the street towards the telegraph office, and he moved quickly to the window, peering out. The three were strolling casually across the dusty street. Angel swore he recognized one of them as Koch, one of Sherman's deputies.

At that precise moment the telegraph began to chatter. Angel spun away from the window. In three long strides he crossed the office and went behind the counter to peer over the telegrapher's shoulder, reading the message as it was written down.

ANGEL. LIBERTY. ARIZONA.

YOUR REPORT ACKNOWLEDGED. STOP. ACTION
UNDERTAKEN. STOP. STAY ALIVE. STOP
ATTORNEY GENERAL.

Angel breathed a sigh of relief. That was the easy
part over with. All he had to do now was to comply
with the Attorney General's request. He stepped
from behind the counter in time to see the three
men step past the window. In a few seconds they
would come in through the door and all hell
would break loose.

Unless. . . .

Angel heard the door creak as someone began
to open it. He lunged across the small office and
went out through the window, head tucked low on
his chest. He hit the boardwalk in a shower of glass
and splintered wood. His momentum took him
across the boardwalk and on to the street. He
rolled, twisting over on to his back so that he was
facing the telegraph office as he came to rest.
Angel still had his gun in his hand and he flipped
it up as he saw figures erupting from the office.
Gunfire split the night. Bullets whacked the dirt
around Angel. He forced himself to sit tight, take
that much longer to aim, then he fired, feeling the
big Colt revolver buck against his palm. He saw
one man bounce back against the office wall, twisting crazily in pain before he went down. Then
Angel was moving, half-crouching, darting along
the street, away from the spill of lamplight cast out
on to the street from the open office door. He felt

the hot burn of a bullet sear his left arm, and he turned viciously, anger drawing his lips back from his clenched teeth in a silent snarl.

Angel's big fist held the Colt steady. He triggered two shots, heard a man scream in agony, clutching both hands to a bloody, ruined face. Blotting out the hideous sounds of pain Angel ran, cutting across the empty street, consciously moving away from the restaurant. He didn't want to draw Cranford's men near the place if he could help it. So where else did he go? At that precise moment Angel didn't really know or care, he simply ran. Only now did he realize that he had left the rifle behind in the telegraph office. There hadn't been time to grab it in his hurry to leave. But he did have the two guns he'd taken from Cranford's men tucked in his belt, plus the Colt he was carrying. He figured he would have to make the best of what he had.

He spotted an alley ahead and went into the darkness. Guns were still firing, He heard a bullet clunk into the wood of the building to his right. White splinters of timber showered him. Angel ran on, stumbling in the darkness. He reached the far end of the alley, turned, and saw dark figures framed in the opening at the far end. Red flickers of flame darted into life. Gunshots rang heavily in the confines of the narrow alley. Angel ducked low, took out one of the other guns, and loosed off a volley of shots. The dark shapes melted away from the mouth of the alley, cursing wildly, but not before one of their number went down howling in agony.

Angel turned along the littered backlots. He moved fast, almost without purpose, and it was with a certain amount of surprise that he found himself crouching in the shadow of Liberty's jail.

As his fingers fed fresh loads into the chambers of his guns Angel's mind was working overtime. Perhaps he hadn't just arrived here at the jail by pure chance. Maybe his subconscious had guided him. After all, the jail was at the centre of this mess. This was where Cranford and Sherman ran their little racket from. So maybe this was where Angel should concentrate his attention. It was a damn good place to hide!

Angel moved swiftly along the side of the jail. As he reached the street frontage he hugged the shadows. Far up the street he could see men moving back and forth. He took a look up at the jail. The boardwalk was empty. Oddly the door stood part-way open. Angel climbed up on to the boardwalk. He stepped quickly to the door, pushed it further open and peered into the office. It looked the same as the last time he'd been in the place.

Except for one thing.

The last time Angel had been in the place, Liberty's Sheriff Phil Sherman had been standing beside the big desk, assisting Judge Cranford.

Sherman was in the office again. But he wasn't standing beside his desk this time. He was on the floor beside the desk, hunched over in an ungainly sprawl. And he was quietly bleeding all over the floor. The blood was coming from a large, pulpy hole in his left shoulder. It didn't take a genius to see that the hole had been caused by a bullet. Which meant that Sherman had been shot. But why – and by whom?'

Angel closed the jail door and locked it. He also slid home the heavy bolts provided. Then he began to check the jail from one end to the other to see if there was anyone else in the building. His search proved fruitless. The cell area was deserted. While he was back there Angel made sure that the jail's rear door was well and truly secured. Then he returned to the office, put down his guns and went to see what he could do for Sherman.

11

'It was Cranford! Double-crossing bastard! He would have killed me, Angel! Christ, he *will* kill me if he gets a chance! I tell you, he's crazy! All because of that money we found in Harry Culp's saddle-bags!'

'You figure that's why he shot you, Sherman?' Angel asked. 'Because of the money. He wants it all?'

Sherman groaned softly as Angel finished tying the crude bandage over the ragged bullet wound. Angel had done what he could to stop the bleeding and clean up the wound. Luck had been on Sherman's side. The bullet had gone clean through his shoulder without touching a bone or major nerves.

'That and the fact I wanted to finish what we got ourselves into. Look, Angel, I was over my head. Cranford was greedy and getting greedier all the time. Even when I told him I'd found out who you were he just laughed it off. Said it was nothing to worry about. He figures he could get us off the hook even if we killed you.' Sherman, his bald head gleaming in the lamplight, stared at Angel. 'Listen, Angel, we ain't going to get out of here alive! Cranford will tear this place apart to get at us.'

'He can try,' Angel murmured. He stood up and crossed the office to inspect the rifles in the rack on the wall behind Sherman's desk.

Sherman had struggled to his feet. He moved slowly to sag heavily into his chair. He watched Angel prowling restlessly around the office.

'No way out, Angel,' he said. 'All the money in the world and it won't do us a damn bit of good!'

Angel spun on his heel. 'What do you mean?'

A frown creased Sherman's drawn face. Then he grinned, showing his large teeth.

'You wouldn't know! I hadn't realized.' He leaned forward. 'Over there in the corner. In that safe!' Sherman almost crowed with delight at his revelation. 'All the goddamn money Cranford and me took is in that safe. Including the pile we got from that Culp feller.'

Angel stood before the safe and studied it. A squat, heavy shape, painted dark green and bolted to the floor. Thick metal strong enough to withstand most attempts at forced entry. Fixed in a central position on the door was a combination lock. Angel stared at the safe angrily. Its presence guaranteed trouble. If what Sherman had said was true, and that safe held a substantial amount of cash, then a visit from Cranford was more than likely. Angel felt like kicking himself. Of all the places in Liberty he had to go and choose this one!

'How did the shooting happen?' Angel asked, rounding on Sherman.

The lawman scowled as he remembered.

'I went over to his house so we could talk. He suggested we come here. I started to get a feeling something was wrong. Cranford was too damn ready to agree with every word I had to say. Time we got in here I was real jumpy. Cranford, he starts getting edgy. Next thing I know he pulls a gun. About the same time he pulls the trigger I heard a lot of shooting up the street.'

'I guess that was me,' Angel admitted.

'Yeah? Well, it put Cranford off. He hit me in the shoulder and I went down. He must have figured he'd killed me. Just 'fore I passed out I heard him run out of here. Next thing I know you turn up.'

'When Cranford can't find me out there he's going to be coming back for his money. Who has the combination?'

'Who do you think,' Sherman growled. 'Cranford. It was his idea to use that safe to keep our money in. Hell, we couldn't go putting it in the bank. Cranford figured the jail was the safest place to keep it.'

Angel crossed to the barred window and stared up the street. Even as he stood there a bunch of armed men appeared from the shadows further along and moved in the direction of the jail.

'Any minute now Cranford's going to find this jail safer for his money than he ever imagined,' Angel said.

'Now wait a minute, Angel,' Sherman protested. 'Are you figuring to stand him off?'

'Well I'm not opening the door and asking him in,' Angel replied. He moved over to the rack of rifles. 'You got the key to this?'

'No!' Sherman said too quickly.

Angel moved to the desk and dragged open drawer after drawer until he found a bunch of keys on a large ring. His third attempt opened the padlock securing a thin chain looped through the trigger guards of the rifles. Angel chose a couple of Winchesters. He had spotted boxes of cartridges in one of the desk drawers. Angel tipped one out on the desk and quickly loaded both rifles. As soon as the job was done Angel crossed to the window again, leaning the rifles against the wall.

'Goddamn!' Sherman exploded. He half-rose from his seat. Sickness rose in his throat and he fell back, groaning from the pain in his shoulder. He was silent for a time. Then he said: 'You can't do this, Angel! It'll get us both killed!'

'What do you expect me to do? Throw him his money – if I could get it out of the damn safe! Get something straight, Sherman. I'm involved in this mess now, so I play it by my rules. I could go through the routine of telling you how I'm empowered legally to take over the law in this town. But I don't have the time. One thing I can tell you – as from now you just resigned as Liberty's sheriff. You're in custody. So is the money in that safe. And I don't hand over anything in my charge. Before I found my way in here I managed to get a telegraph message to my people in Washington. They know all about the mess this town's in and they're sending help.'

'What the hell do you expect Cranford to do? Stand and wait? Jesus, Angel, he'll shoot us full of holes before he rides off with his money!'

Angel smiled. 'First he has to get to it.'

'You don't know Amos Cranford like I do. He's a crafty son of a bitch. I tell you, Angel, he'll find a way in to us!'

'Let me worry about that,' Angel said, and returned to the window.

He spotted Cranford first. The man was standing in a pool of yellow lamplight, in the act of stepping up on to the boardwalk outside the jail.

Angel raised the catch on the window and silently pushed it open.

'I was you, Cranford, I wouldn't come any higher!'

Cranford stopped, head jerking to one side, eyes narrowed as he stared in the direction of the voice.

'Phil, that you?'

'It's me, Cranford, Frank Angel. You want something?'

Silence. Angel could almost put himself in Cranford's place. His mind ticking over, evaluating the new set of circumstances. Figuring a way so that things came out in his favour.

'Son of a bitch!' Cranford said with great relish. 'All right, Mister Justice Department Angel, what do you want?'

'I'd be satisfied with you and your hired guns in these empty cells.'

'Go to hell, Angel!' A harsh voice hurled out of the shadows behind Cranford. It was easily recognizable. Trench – the boss of the prison.

'Trench, shut up!' Cranford snapped. To Angel he said: 'Angel, you know what's in that safe? It's mine and I'm not leaving Liberty without it.'

'Appears to me you've got yourself a problem then – Judge!'

'No, boy, the problem's yours. You're alone, in my town, and you don't stand a chance!'

'I'll take it the way it comes,' Angel said. 'Cranford, you know damn well I've been in touch with my people in Washington. I'm not going to be alone for long!'

Cranford laughed at that. 'Pure horseshit, Angels, and I'm not fool enough to panic over it. We're a long way from anywhere. It's going to be days before they can get help to you. How're you figuring on staying alive that long?'

'Don't know any better, Judge. Nobody ever taught me about quitting!'

A low moan came from Phil Sherman. He struggled clumsily to his feet, knocking over his chair. 'Christ, Angel, I never figured on anything like this! He's got us boxed in good and tight! You can't hold out against that bunch!'

'We'll find out one way or another,' Angel remarked.

'Angel!' Cranford yelled. 'You got Phil Sherman in there with you? Is that bastard still alive?'

'He's alive,' Angel confirmed. 'You're one hell of a lousy shot, Cranford. But I'm grateful. See, Sherman's so mad at you he's making a full confession. Putting it all down on paper. Every detail of every dirty trick you pulled. It'll make good evidence for your trial!'

'Trial? What damn trial, Angel? Not mine. I'll see you in hell first!'

'Damn you, Angel, we'll never get out of here alive,' Sherman groaned. 'What did you want to go and mention a trial for?'

'Because that's what Cranford's heading for,' Angel said.

'No chance,' Sherman replied. His face paled abruptly. 'You've got to get me out of this, Angel. It's your job to see I don't get killed!'

Sherman spotted the cold expression that drifted across Angel's face too late. He tried to step back, but Angel's right hand, palm open, caught him across the side of the face. The sound of the blow was loud in the office. Sherman stumbled back, biting back any words ready to spring from his lips. He realized how close he'd come to getting himself killed by the very man who might save him.

'I was you, Sherman, I'd be careful what I said,'

Angel warned. 'Seems to me you could have been thinking along those lines when you let Harry Culp die.'

'That was Cranford and Trench,' Sherman protested. 'Weren't a thing I could have done to have stopped that! It's easy for you to say how things should have been, Angel. You weren't mixed up with Cranford! I was!'

'Sure, it just happened. You bastards are all the same. The minute you get caught you start bleating about not being responsible. It wasn't your fault. You didn't know what was going on. Well, hard shit, Sherman, you won't get any sympathy from me. Don't forget I happened to go through your little set-up and I didn't see anybody forcing you to play your part. And you damn well seemed to know what was going on. How do you explain that?'

Sherman remained silent. He had no way out of that. Angel had him cold and Sherman knew it.

'Sherman, you know the situation we're in. I'll do what I can to keep us both alive. But I want help from you on one thing. I told Cranford you were putting everything down on paper. That's just what I do want you to do. Just in case something happens I want a record of Cranford's activities. You can put down how you were involved too, and when you've finished, sign and date it.'

'You really mean it,' Sherman scowled. 'All right, Angel, what if I co-operate — tell me how much it's worth! If I'm going to give you the

109

evidence you need to get Cranford, what's in it for me?'

Angel smiled. 'Lucky for you, Sherman, that will be up to somebody else. If I had my say you'd be a dead man right now! So find yourself a pen and some paper and get to work. There might not be much time, I have a feeling Cranford's going to start getting impatient pretty soon.'

In fact Amos Cranford's patience ran out after exactly thirty minutes.

12

Cranford's men hit the jail front and rear. The interior of the building echoed to the blast of gunfire. The front window exploded inwards, glass and shredded wood showering the office. Bullets whined across the room, expending themselves in the thick adobe-and-stone walls. While the gunfire carried on, other men made attempts to break down the front and rear doors. They retreated after a couple of minutes. Shortly after that the gunfire ceased and it became ominously quiet.

Raising his head from below the edge of his desk Sherman glanced across the office to where Angel stood.

'Ain't you going to do anything?' Sherman demanded.

Angel glanced at him.

'Time'll come,' he said. 'Right now they've found out it ain't going to be easy getting in here. It didn't do us any harm but they used a lot of

111

ammunition and energy. Next time they'll try something else.'

He crossed to the window and peered out through the bars. At first glance the street appeared empty. Over on the far side, though, Angel was able to make out the dark shapes of waiting men. They were huddled together in a tight bunch. Trying to decide on their next move. Angel settled himself against the wall beside the window and waited.

'Angel!'

'Yeah?'

'Why don't we get the hell out of here before they come again?'

Angel glanced over his shoulder at Sherman. Liberty's lawman was hunched over his desk, staring down at the paper he was writing on.

'How do you plan for us to do that, Sherman? You can bet your last dollar Cranford's got front and back covered. Maybe you're planning for us to fly out!'

Sherman's head rose with a jerk. He stared vacantly at Angel, as if he had just roused himself from a deep sleep.

'Guess I ain't thinking too straight,' he said, unable to conceal the nervous tremor in his voice.

'Just let it lie,' Angel told him. 'We'll take our chance when it comes!'

He turned back to the window in time to see the knot of men break apart. He noticed, too, that there were many lamplight reflections beginning

112

to show along the street. The citizens of Liberty were having their evening calm disrupted, yet nobody seemed interested enough to venture out on to the street to investigate.

'Angel! Angel, you hear me?'

Amos Cranford's voice floated out of the shadows.

'I hear you.'

'Angel, don't be a fool! You can't win, man! See reason, Angel, give up. Let me have what I want and you and Sherman can walk away unharmed!'

Sherman himself gave a hollow laugh. He stood up and came to stand beside Angel at the window.

'Think about it, Angel,' Cranford advised. 'Wouldn't you rather stay alive?'

'Sure we would, Amos,' Sherman yelled. 'That's why we ain't about to listen to any of your deals!'

Cranford swore volubly.

'You want it the hard way, so that's how it's going to be!' There was unconcealed rage in Cranford's tone now. 'You're both fools and in a while you'll be dead fools!'

Sherman uttered a low sigh.

'Much as I hate to admit it, Angel, I got to agree with him. We're as good as dead right now. Christ, man, he's got us and he knows it!'

'You see it any way you want to, Sherman,' Angel said. 'I ain't dead yet – 'cause if I am I'm the liveliest corpse you're ever going to see!'

Cranford retraced his steps to the far side of the

street and for a time nothing appeared to be happening.

Maintaining his position at the window Angel kept his eyes on the tight group of men. He knew damn well that they were up to something, and he would have given a month's pay to know what it was.

Without warning a horse and rider came out of an alley on Cranford's side of the street. At first Angel couldn't understand the reasoning behind the move. The rider was half-way across the street before Angel realized what was happening. His keen eyes picked out the red tracery of sparks falling away behind the rider. The sparks came from a dark bundle in the rider's hand. Angel's mind whirled frantically, and then it hit him.

Explosives!

The bastards were going to blow the goddamn jail apart to get at him!

Angel jerked his rifle up, aiming and firing in a single motion. The blast of the Winchester was loud in the comparative silence. The rider went back out of his saddle like he'd been hit with a forty-foot plank. But his right arm had already reached the apex of its swing as he arched violently off the horse. Angel watched the dark bundle leave the rider's hand. Saw the glowing red tail. He watched for a second, held by the awful directness of the bundle's trajectory, and knew that he had to got away from the front of the jail.

And fast!

He pushed himself away from the window, throwing out a hand to shove Sherman aside. His palm touched Sherman's chest. Angel shoved hard, feeling a warning yell rising in his throat. Yet he knew, coldly, logically, that it was too late.

Far too late.

The front wall of the jail vanished in a blinding flare of flame. Thick coils of smoke and dust gushed into the office. The ear-splitting roar of the explosion mingled with the crash of falling masonry and splintering timber.

Angel, half-way across the office, was lifted off his feet as though he was weightless. The explosion threw him across the room, slamming him brutally up against the far wall. A fragmentary burst of pain preceded a total blackout. Angel felt nothing as a mass of stone and timber piled up over his inert body.

He heard nothing. Saw nothing. Felt nothing.

He lay like the dead – and because of that he stayed alive.

13

Angel woke up with a sullen headache, countless cuts and bruises, but no serious injuries. Liberty's former lawman, Phil Sherman, however had not been so lucky. He had died as a result of the explosion, so Liberty's doctor informed Angel. He imparted this information while he was treating Angel in a small, neat bedroom which turned out to be situated over Jessica Blake's restaurant. The doctor was a gruff, dark-haired man in his late forties. He had an abrasive manner, a brown, seamed face, and hands as gentle as a woman's. He wore a pair of steel-rimmed spectacles that clung by some miracle to the extreme tip of his nose, and he peered over the rims at his patient as he tended to the various wounds covering Angel's torso.

'You people just have no consideration,' the doctor grumbled. 'Never a thought, day or night, when you set out on these damn shooting-matches!' He paused in his ministrations to stare accusingly at Angel. 'You listening to me, boy?'

Angel smiled painfully. 'I'm all ears, Doc.'

'And you can cut out the facetious remarks, too, young feller. Ain't it enough I get dragged out of bed in the middle of the night to tend your damn-fool hurts? Insults I don't need. Department of Justice, eh? Seems to me they must be in a bad way if they have to take you so young.'

'Sign of the times, Doc,' Angel said. 'It's a young man's world!'

The doctor gave a bandage an unnecessarily hard turn over Angel's ribs. Angel winced. The doctor ignored his patient's discomfort and carried on.

'I suppose it's a waste of time telling you to rest?'

Angel nodded, 'Sorry, Doc. Soon as I can stand up without falling on my face I've got to move out.'

'What happens to Cranford when you catch him?'

'Not up to me to decide.' Angel sat up at the doctor's request. 'All I have to do is find him and bring him back.'

'They ought to hang the son of a bitch!' the doctor said with surprising venom.

'That's likely.'

The doctor finished his handiwork.

'If you have to go riding all over the territory, boy, just remember what happened to you a short time ago. The body needs time to recover. I doubt yours will get that but try and remember all the same.'

'Thanks, Doc, I'll try and take it easy,' Angel promised.

The doctor put away his tackle and closed his bag. At the door he paused, turned, staring over his spectacles at Angel.

'One thing, boy, who the hell pays my bill?'

Angel stood up, carefully flexing muscles and limbs. With a little care, he realized, he might be able to move small distances over long periods of time.

'Send it to the Department of Justice in Washington,' he suggested to the medical man.

'Don't think I won't!' The doctor closed the door firmly behind him when he left.

Angel spent a few minutes walking round and round the confines of the room. He felt a little unsteady at first but after a couple of circuits he had regained control of his wandering balance. He was still working flexibility into his stiff joints when somebody tapped on the door.

'Come on in.'

The door opened to reveal Jess Blake. She had a cup of black coffee in one hand and a man's shirt draped over her arm. She smiled at Angel and passed him the shirt.

'Best I could do at this time of night,' she said.

Angel pulled the shirt on and found that it fitted him perfectly. He took the coffee Jess offered.

'How do you feel now?' she enquired.

'Let's say I've had better days.'

'We thought you were dead. There was so much

118

confusion at the jail after Cranford and his men left. Everybody was crowding round, shouting orders to each other. We found Phil Sherman first – or what was left of him. It was Birdy who found you. He practically dug you out with his bare hands.'

'Where is he?' Angel asked.

'After we'd got you up here and the doctor said you weren't badly hurt, Birdy took his horse and told me to tell you he was going to follow Cranford. Keep the trail in sight he said.'

'Damn!' Angel swore. He quickly downed the remainder of his coffee. 'Jess, I've got to move fast. The last thing Birdy should be doing is trailing Cranford and his bunch. He's no tracker and he certainly isn't a gunman!'

'I said the same but he seemed to want to do it,' Jess said. 'I hope he'll be all right.'

Angel's thoughts ran along the same lines. He just hoped that Birdy had the good sense to keep his activities restricted to no more than simply tracking Cranford and his bunch. If he was spotted Birdy wouldn't stand a chance against Cranford's hired guns.

While Jess made up a sack of food Angel went across to the wrecked jail. Only now, by the light of a couple of lanterns which had been rigged up, was he able to see the extent of the damage. The explosive charge had knocked down most of the front wall and part of the roof. Ignoring the curious stares of the men in and around the jail Angel clambered over the rubble until he could get to Sherman's desk. He dragged open the drawers one by one. In the last drawer he found what he was looking for. His own gunbelt and Colt. Angel checked the gun and then strapped on the belt. He noticed that the rifles were still in the wall rack. For the second time that night he chose a weapon. There were still plenty of cartridges for the rifle in the desk. Angel loaded the rifle and shoved a handful of spare cartridges in his pocket.

Angel left the jail and walked down the street to the livery stable which, Jess had explained, looked after the horses of Liberty's law-force. Also, she told him, the stable housed any livestock belonging to prisoners. The livery owner grumbled long and loud when Angel knocked him up and told him he wanted his horse. The man began to assume a belligerent pose until Angel shoved his badge under the man's nose. The protests stopped as if the man had suddenly suffered a cut throat. He dragged on a pair of pants and led Angel to the stable. Inside, Angel quickly located his horse and gear. He saddled up and led the horse outside, mounted up, and rode through town to Jess Blake's restaurant. She came outside with the food she had put in a sack.

'It seems silly, but take care,' she said, smiling up at him,

Angel tied the sack of food behind his saddle.

'I will, Jess, and thanks. Now just point me in the right direction.'

'They rode north,' Jess told him.

Raising a swift hand Angel turned his horse about and rode away from Liberty. He knew that in a few hours it would be light. Once daylight came Birdy was going to find difficulty concealing himself from Cranford's bunch. They were going to be on the look-out for any kind of pursuit. If they saw Birdy, and recognized him, Angel knew very well that they wouldn't hesitate to kill him.

He tried to work out where Cranford might be making for. The man had a lot of money with him – Angel hadn't missed seeing the open safe in the wreck of the jail – and it would help him to go far. Cranford might carry on to the far north, up into Canada. Then again he could cut west towards California, taking the lonely trails across the High Sierras. He could just as easily make for one of the railroads, buy himself a ticket and go in any one of half a dozen directions. There was a lot of country available for Cranford to choose from. Nor was he even restricted to the United States. San Francisco, for instance, offered the opportunity for someone with money to book passage on any number of passenger ships bound for foreign ports. Likewise the eastern seaboard provided similar facilities. There was even South America. A man with Amos Cranford's talent for nefarious activities could easily carve himself a comfortable niche in one of those steamy, isolated, tropical little republics down at the far end of the Latin American continent. With his knowledge of law and his money,

Cranford had the means of rising to great heights, no matter how dubious his motivations and his methods.

With Liberty dropping further and further behind him Angel pushed his horse deeper into the bleak, dark slopes of the hills above the town. He rode as fast as he could while still managing to follow the faint trail left by Cranford's bunch, and the single line of tracks Birdy was producing. The silent hours drifted by in a blur. And slowly, imperceptibly at first, the deep-night hue of the sky began to fade. Pale streaks of light began to break the monotony of the darkness. There was little change in the temperature. Angel found himself shivering slightly against the keen chill of the high country. In a few hours he would be longing for its return. With the eventual rising of the sun would come the endless hours of savage heat. The air thick, cloying. The vaulted canyons and rocky escarpments would become vast, unrelenting ovens, reflecting the trapped heat with magnified intensity.

Angel crested a high ridge, reining in his panting horse. He slipped from the saddle and gave the animal a few minutes' rest. He took his canteen and swallowed a mouthful of cold water. While his horse took the opportunity to chew at some clumps of tough grass, Angel made use of the halt to study the landscape. Early-morning light was flooding the land, washing the earth and rocks with its sheer brilliance. At this height the altitude created a clearness in the air that added to the natural capabilities of man's eyesight. Angel found he was able to pick out far-distant objects with startling clarity.

Like the riderless horse wandering aimlessly across the face of the long slope far above him, Angel watched the horse for a while, aware of a growing sensation of unease settling over him. Abruptly he went to his horse and mounted up. He kicked the animal into motion, yanking impatiently at the reins when the horse showed signs of reluctance at being disturbed. Once he was moving Angel pushed his horse hard.

Even so it took him almost an hour to reach the spot where he'd first seen the riderless horse. He followed the tracks it had left. He found the animal a few minutes later, grazing in the shade of some rooks. It was the same horse Birdy had used on the ride into Liberty. Angel gathered the resins and led the horse as he rode back the way it had come, following the line of erratic hoofprints it had left.

He found Birdy face down at the base of a granite rockface. Even before he climbed from his saddle Angel was able to see the ugly, criss-cross weals and tears in Birdy's body. The man's clothing was in bloody shreds. Angel knew what had caused them. He'd seen the results of brutal whippings before. A man skilled in the use of those ugly weapons could tear flesh from bone. And Angel didn't doubt Trench's capabilities one little bit.

'Oh . . . oh . . . God it hurts!'

Birdy's thin body began to shudder violently as Angel turned him over. The skinny man's chest and face were torn and bloody. Deep gashes left white bone exposed in a number of places. Birdy stared up at Angel as if he was a stranger, then recognition shone in his dull eyes and he clutched at Angel's arm with a bloody hand.

'I knew you'd come, Angel. Didn't figure on getting caught, mind. But one of Cranford's boys must have spotted me. Hell, I ain't no damn Apache. Anyhow they snuck up on me 'fore I knew what was happening. They wanted to know if anybody else was following. I told 'em there wasn't. Funny thing is they didn't believe me an' it was the truth. So that son of a bitch Trench laid into me with that whip.' Birdy paused for a while, biting back the pain rising in his body.

'Jesus, Angel, I never knew a man could hurt so much and not be dead. That bastard Trench, he really let go at me. Hell, I figured I'd done pretty good while they had me in that camp. All that time and I never once felt that whip. Minute I get out who do I walk right into! I told you I wasn't safe on my own, Angel.'

'I wish you'd have told me what you were up to,' Angel said. 'It was a dumb thing to do, Birdy, taking off after Cranford on your own.'

'Yeah, I found that out,' Birdy whispered. 'I just figured you needed a little help, Angel.'

'Don't think I'm not grateful, Birdy. I just wish it

hadn't cost you so much.'

Birdy nodded. 'What the hell, Angel. I had nowhere else to go. But I did all right for you? Didn't I, Angel?'

Angel nodded. 'Sure, Birdy, you did fine. They won't get away now.'

Angel made no mention of the fact that he would have been able to pick up Cranford's trail without Birdy's help. Whatever Birdy's motivation for wanting to help Angel it had only brought him pain and suffering. To reveal that his efforts had been unnecessary would have been as harsh as allowing further punishment from Trench's whip.

'Birdy, how many of them are there?' Angel asked.

'Cranford, Trench. That pair who used to be Sherman's deputies . . . Duggan and Koch. And a couple of the guards from the camp. I figure Cranford must have paid off the rest of them.' Birdy managed a faint grin. 'That too many for you, Angel?'

'Kind of odds I usually take care of before breakfast.'

'Yeah. Hell, Angel, I wish I could see you. . . !'

Birdy's voice trailed off. When Angel glanced down at him, the man was dead.

Angel slid the body into a shallow depression in the ground and covered it with rocks. He unsaddled Birdy's horse and turned it loose. He placed Birdy's handgun in his saddle-bags, hung the canteen from his saddle horn. Then he mounted up and put his horse on the trail. He did not look back at Birdy's lonely grave, simply stared ahead, his whole being focused on what lay before him.

14

There was a saying to the effect that you never heard the bullet with your name on it. If the saying was true, Angel decided, then somebody had misspelt his name, because he very definitely heard the bullet – and felt its passing. Angel left his saddle without hesitation, snatching for the rifle in the scabbard at his side. He hit the ground on his left shoulder, hugging the Winchester to his body as he rolled towards the scant cover of a flat boulder. Almost separately a section of his mind was registering the flat crackle of further shots. Bullets whacked the rocky ground, howling off into the air. As far as Angel could judge there were at least two rifles.

Angel hit the base of the boulder. Putting more strain on his battered muscles than his condition warranted, Angel thrust his body over the top of the boulder. He was already rolling towards the far side when yet another shot sounded. Angel gave a soft grunt of pain as the bullet ripped a bloody gouge across his left shoulder. He felt hot blood coursing down his back as he tumbled behind the boulder. Fighting off the surge of pain and nausea, Angel twisted round, bringing the Winchester to his shoulder.

He scanned the rocky slopes above his position. Nothing showed at first. Angel waited patiently, just hoping that whoever was up in those rocks lacked that quality. Sunlight flickered along the exposed barrel of a rifle. Angel shifted his position slightly. The rifleman, above him and to his left, seemed also to be on the move. Angel gave him a few more seconds. Then he caught a glimpse of the man's dark bulk, could even make out the pale oval of the face.

'All right, you son of a bitch,' Angel breathed. He angled the Winchester, held his target and allowed for the rise of the slope before he touched the trigger. The Winchester cracked, muzzle lifting in recoil. His bullet struck within a half-inch of Angel's intended mark, throwing the rifleman back off his feet.

Angel levered a fresh round into the breech, gasping as the sudden movement caused an ugly shaft of pain to burn across his shoulder. He sagged against the boulder, swearing softly. It did little to ease the pain but it still made Angel feel a whole lot better.

Somewhere above him hoofs clattered on hard rock. A shower of loose stone shot down the dusty slope, pin-pointing the whereabouts of the second rifleman. It appeared that he'd had enough and was leaving.

Angel came to his feet, bursting out from behind the boulder, searching the sunbright slope above him. He was angry enough to allow his caution to slip. A surge of recklessness took control. He ran across the open ground, stumbling in his haste.

The rider broke into view, coming down the treacherous slope at breakneck speed. His face, a white blur, was turned towards Angel. As he realized Angel's potential threat, the rider made a desperate shot with the rifle held in his right hand. He yanked the weapon across his body, wasting precious seconds before he pulled the trigger.

Angel was already diving towards the ground, his own rifle lifting as he hit the hard earth. He heard the other rifle explode, the shot passing over his prone body. Angel returned fire, came to his feet, and fired again. He saw his bullets hit, ripping bloody holes in the rider's body. The man went limp and rolled loosely from his saddle. He hit the slope face down, slithering in a floppy sprawl and coming to rest at the bottom.

Angel came to a dead stop. He remained motionless for a time, watching and listening, his wild anger subsiding gradually. Movement off to one side brought the Winchester up, but it was only one of the horses. Angel eyed the wandering animal as he let the rifle sag. He crossed to where his own horse was standing. He sheathed his rifle and reached for his canteen, noticing the fresh blood running across his left hand. He became aware now of the sharp sting of pain across his shoulder. Blood had soaked the back of his shirt and sleeve. With the wound in the place it was there wasn't much he could do about it. So Angel ignored it.

He mounted up a few minutes later and rode on. It didn't take him long to pick up the trail again, just beyond the rise of low hills before him.

Cranford had chosen his spot well, Angel had to admit. The man had wanted to make certain that if anyone was following they would maybe have second thoughts if a few of them were killed. If it hadn't been for that poor opening shot the matter might have had a totally different outcome. As it was Cranford had lost two men, and Angel had lessened the odds from six to four.

Angel pushed his horse as hard as he dare. The day was living up to the promise shown in the early hours. The cloudless sky poured down endless waves of brutal sunlight. The heat was almost overpowering. It became trapped in the rocks, glaring up off the bleached earth. It hung in shimmering curtains before his aching eyes, causing the very landscape to tremble and waver.

Somewhere close by he heard a faint sound. Angel reined in and listened. He unsheathed his rifle. The sound came again, a soft rattle. Angel climbed down from his horse and moved toward the mass of boulders and choked brush from where the sound was emanating.

He found a horse, down on the ground, one of its forelegs badly broken. Splintered bone gleamed white where it had pierced the flesh. Angel put a quick shot through the horse's head, ending its misery. Now they were four with only three horses. One mount would have to carry double. Angel gazed down at the dead horse. Cranford was going to find his progress slowed down considerably.

Angel returned to his horse and put it back on the trail. The tracks he was following began to angle off towards the east. Coming down off a high slope Angel caught a flash of greenery and a short while later he was riding through tall stands of aspen and spruce. The ground underfoot here was soft, thick with leaf mould and the trail was clearer than it had been for any time since he had first picked it up. Angel could easily see the deeper marks made by the horse carrying double.

Shortly after noon Angel broke out of the trees and drew rein. Just below him, on the bank of a wide, meandering creek, stood a low, rambling log building. Smoke curled lazily from the stone chimney. Chickens moved back and forth across the trampled yard. Horses stamped restlessly around the small corral. Angel studied the place for a time. It looked peaceful enough. But he knew of old that it was this sort of place that generally gave the most trouble. He rode in with caution, his rifle across his thighs. As he drew nearer the place he saw the weathered sign over the door: ANDER-SON'S POST. Angel wondered idly how long the place had existed. Thirty? Maybe forty years? Possibly even longer. There were hundreds of these places dotted around the country. In the early days, long before any towns had been estab-lished, these isolated trading posts had been the only contact with other white men that had existed for the early explorers. A place for them to buy supplies. To sell their furs. To come in out of the wilderness simply to see and speak to others of their kind. The posts had been places of contact between the Indians and the whites. They were generally considered safe places by the Indians, and were left alone even during times of hostility. Not always – but for the most part the posts survived.

Angel crossed the yard and took a quick look in the corral. He easily spotted the single horse, standing motionless amongst the other restless animals. Angel dismounted, led his horse over to the corral and tied it to one of the posts. He slipped through the bars and crossed the corral to the horse he'd spotted. The animal didn't even back off when he approached. Angel gave it a quick look over. Its lower legs were dust-stained. Its coat was still lathered and damp. Angel made his way out of the corral, certain that he had found two of his men.

He left his rifle in its sheath, checking his Colt before he made for the post. At the door he paused, giving his eyes time to adjust to the interior light. Then he stepped inside quickly.

The main room was large, low-ceilinged. The section nearer to the door held all the trading goods, foodstuffs. Down at the far end was a section that had been turned into a small saloon-cum-dining-room, A row of shelves held an assortment of bottles. A couple of casks were supported on wood blocks. Fronting this was the bar, consisting of three thick, rough-hewn planks laid across large barrels. Behind the bar was a lean, hawk-faced man in his late forties. He had thick, red hair, the kind that stuck out from his head in unruly tangles, defying any attempt at keeping it tidy. He was dressed in dark pants and a rose-coloured shirt. He was deeply absorbed in rolling himself a cigarette, so he didn't notice Angel's appearance.

Nor did his only customers: two travel-stained men at the bar, hunched over their drinks in sullen silence. Duggan and Koch. The two ex-deputies from Liberty.

'Just stay where you are, boys, and we can do this without anybody getting hurt,' Angel said. He spoke evenly, making certain there was no threat in his tone.

The man behind the bar glanced in Angel's direction. He took one look at the tall, unshaven, battered figure standing there, and decided not to interfere.

'You hear me?' Angel asked.

133

'That you, Angel?' Koch asked over his shoulder.

'Yeah!'

Koch laughed. 'We should of killed you when we had the chance. I reckon if we had we wouldn't be in this damn mess right now!'

'Judge gone and run out on you?'

Koch emptied his glass with an angry gesture.

'Too true, Angel. He just upped and paid us off. Said it was time to go our own ways.'

'Weren't my fault the goddamn horse broke a leg!' Duggan's voice was high with self-pity.

'For Christ' sake, shut your mouth about that horse! Nobody said it was your fault.'

Duggan grunted something. 'It sure as hell is what you're thinkin',' he threw out.

'Balls!' Koch muttered. He turned slowly from the bar to face Angel. 'One thing we better get straight, Angel, from here on in. I ain't about to turn in my gun and go with you! No way, mister.'

'Koch, it's up to you,' Angel told him. 'Makes no difference to me. I can deliver you either way. Dead or Alive!'

'Go to hell, Angel!' Koch yelled. 'I don't figure on ending up behind bars! Or dancing on the end of a rope! No chance, Angel, so I'll just have to kill you myself!'

And as he spoke Koch went for his holstered gun and started shooting.

15

Fast as Koch was, Angel turned out to be faster. He barely seemed to move, yet the big Colt was suddenly in his hand. It was level and it was aimed at Koch's chest. Koch had already fired off two shots. One smashed into the edge of the bar near Angel's right elbow. The other tore through the log roof overhead, because Koch's gun had tilted in that direction as Angel's bullet took him just over the heart. Koch went over backwards, letting go with a loud scream of pain that trailed off to a soft whimper. His limp body slumped against one of the barrels supporting the bar. Koch lay with his head flopping forward, seeming to stare at the blood pumping out of the hole in his chest.

'The hell with you, Angel!' Duggan roared. He had started to turn even while Angel and Koch were trading shots. His gun was half-way out of his holster as Koch went down. Angel saw that Duggan was going to start shooting a little ahead of himself, so he moved, wanting to alter his position.

That would mean Duggan having to aim again and it would give Angel the precious seconds he required.

Angel dropped to the floor, letting his body roll. He heard the solid thunder of sound as Duggan fired, heard the thwack as the bullet chewed a long sliver of wood from the floor.

'Jesus, will you stand still and fight!' Duggan yelled. He half-turned, swinging his gun round.

Angel fired from where he lay. His bullet caught Duggan in the left shoulder, spinning the big man around. Duggan's legs became entangled in the legs of a chair and he crashed to the floor in a bloody heap. He kicked the chair aside and staggered to his feet. He sighted Angel, in the act of rising, and brought up his gun again, triggering wild shots in Angel's direction. One bullet burned across the back of Angel's hand. And then Angel's gun crashed again, and again. Duggan gave a stunned grunt, his body shuddering under the impact of the heavy bullets. Blood began to stain his shirt, soaking his pants. He stumbled drunkenly, desperately trying to stay on his feet. But his body had taken too much punishment. As his left leg lost all feeling Duggan arced to the floor. He twisted over on to his back, blood marking the worn boards. His left boot-heel drummed spasmodically on the floor. He opened his mouth, perhaps to speak, but any words were lost in the rise of blood gushing from his throat.

Angel climbed to his feet and deliberately

reloaded his Colt before he did anything else.

'Hey . . . Angel. . . !'

Angel knelt beside Koch. The man was staring at him with half-closed eyes. A slippery sheen of blood coated his chest and the hands he had clasped over the wound. A thin trickle showed at the corner of his mouth.

'You knew damn well we wouldn't let you take us in,' Koch whispered. The effort of a continuous sentence left him breathless.

'A stupid move, Koch,' Angel said.

Koch shrugged slightly. 'Yeah. Well . . . I . . . never did much thinkin'.'

'Koch, you want to tell me where Cranford's heading?'

'Save my soul?' Koch gave a hoarse chuckle. 'Too . . . too . . . damn late . . . for that . . . Angel. What the hell . . . I don't owe that bastard a thing . . . no way. Him an' Trench . . . they's headin' . . . for . . . Marcos . . .' Koch began to cough. Mainly he coughed up blood, and when he stopped coughing he was dead.

Standing at the bar Angel eyed the red-haired man. The man picked up a bottle and a glass, gesturing in Angel's direction.

'Looks like a good idea,' Angel said.

'Personal quarrel?' the man asked as he poured Angel a drink.

Angel fished out his badge and laid it on the bar. The man studied it for a while, craning his neck to read all the words inscribed around the rim.

'That make you a marshal?'

'Investigator,' Angel told him.

The man held out his hand. 'Name's Loomis. Jack Loomis.'

'Frank Angel.'

'Anything I can do for you, Mr Angel?'

'Tell me where Marcos is.'

'Ain't nothing to tell. It's just a scrubby little cow-town half a day's ride east of here.'

So why was Cranford making for it? Angel emptied his glass and placed it on the bar. Loomis refilled it automatically.

'Anything special about Marcos?'

Loomis shook his head.

'Not a damn thing. If it wasn't for the spurline I don't reckon Marcos would even be there.'

Angel's head came up with a jerk.

'Spurline? To where?'

'Why, the Santa Fe.'

Angel nodded. That was Cranford's way out. He would ride the spurline to where it merged with the main Atchison, Topeka and Santa Fe line. From there he could board any of the long haul express trains which ran between Chicago and Los Angeles on the west coast. Cranford could take his pick of trains. He could go east or west, even change direction if he desired.

'Mr Loomis, I'd like a fresh horse. Seems I got me some hard riding to do.'

Loomis nodded. 'Come on out to the corral.'

'How long have that other pair been gone?'

'Around three hours.'

'There should be money enough on that pair to bury them,' Angel said as they stepped outside. 'I'd stop and lend a hand if I hadn't pressing business in Marcos.'

Loomis smiled. 'Don't you worry on that score, Mr Angel. I'll plant those two and put markers over them.'

'Thanks, Mr Loomis,' Angel said. 'You are a gentleman.'

'There ain't many of us left, Mr Angel, and that's a pure fact.'

16

They came to Marcos as darkness fell. A chill wind was rolling down off the high peaks and heavy clouds were filling the sky. The first rain began to fall as they took their horses up the single, rutted main street of the small town.

Amos Cranford eased his stiff body from the saddle, leading his horse the last few steps to the hitching rail outside the single-storey building that served as the rail depot booking and dispatch office. Some way up the single set of tracks stood slatted holding-pens, there for the cattle Marcos sent to the outside world. There was little else.

'Let me see to the tickets, then we can go and get something to eat,' he said to Trench.

Cranford strolled round to the front of the booking office. He peered in through the glass-paned door, relieved to see that there was some-one seated behind the counter. He opened the door and went in. Warmth from a glowing stove in one corner of the room rushed out to meet him.

Cranford closed the door. As he crossed the floor he heard a sudden heavy downpour of rain.

'Damn and blast this weather!'

The speaker was the booking-clerk, seated behind the counter. He stared out of one of the windows, wrinkling his face as he watched the rain streaming down the glass. He was an old man, dressed in a worn black uniform. He had a green eyeshade over his eyes and he turned to glare at Cranford.

'What do you want, feller?' he demanded.

'Couple of tickets on the next train out,' Cranford said.

'Where to, feller?' the old man asked.

'We want to pick up one of the mainline expresses. So I want the tickets to get us there.'

The old man muttered to himself. He slid off his stool and went to the shelf at the back of the counter.

'Flagstaff!' he said loudly.

'What?'

The old man stared at Cranford as if he was dealing with some kind of geriatric idiot.

'Flagstaff, feller! That's where the train'll take you so you can make your connection!'

Cranford nodded. 'All right. Two tickets to Flagstaff. How much?'

The old man consulted a worn book. Eventually he worked out the price. Cranford paid and put away the tickets.

'What time does the train leave?'

The old man glanced at the big clock on the wall above his counter. 'Eight o'clock on the button,' he announced. 'That is, providing there ain't any delays.'

'Gives us time for a meal,' Cranford remarked as he made for the door.

'Gives you time for more than that, feller,' the old man said, smiling for the first time. 'That's eight o'clock tomorrow morning. Ain't no train leaving Marcos tonight, feller, so there ain't no call for you to hurry!'

Cranford left the booking-office and banged the door shut behind him. He ran to where Trench was waiting with the horses.

'How long we got to wait?' Trench asked as Crahford mounted up.

'All damn night,' Cranford told him. 'There isn't a train out of here until eight in the morning.'

They rode back uptown, bodies hunched against the rain slanting in along the street. Lamps were already being lit against the rapidly approaching gloom.

'At least we can sleep in a bed tonight,' Trench pointed out.

Cranford saw little comfort in the revelation. He would have preferred to have been moving rapidly away from this part of the country. The longer he stayed the more possible became the chance of his capture. The man named Angel, whether dead or not, had set in motion the machine he worked for. Cranford knew enough about the Justice

Department to realize that they would have Liberty sealed off before very long. Once that happened they would start digging and it would come to light, sooner or later, how Cranford had been running his operation. Before that happened Amos Cranford wanted to be far, far away.

'Hotel!' Trench's monosyllabic tone brought Cranford out of his thoughts.

'It'll do,' Cranford said.

They dismounted and tied the horses. Cranford freed his fat saddle-bags and hung them over his shoulder. He intended sleeping with them next to him. His future was in those pouches and he in no way wanted to take any chance of losing that.

They walked into the hotel lobby, shaking the rain from their clothing. The place was dusty and nondescript. Cranford walked to the desk and thumped his fist hard down on the top. A young clerk, with an oval face and an overweight body, emerged from the office in back of the desk. He had oily skin and dark hair of the kind that hung limply over his face.

'Couple of single rooms,' Cranford said. 'Just for the night. We'll be leaving on the eight o'clock train in the morning.'

'You'all like to sign the book,' the clerk drawled. He watched with total disinterest as Cranford signed the register.

'I'll pay now,' Cranford said, 'so there won't be any delay in the morning.'

'Sure. Rooms are two dollars each.'

Cranford paid, took the keys the clerk handed him, and led the way up the creaking stairs. He took the first room for himself and gave Trench the other key.

'Give me ten minutes to clean up and we'll go eat,' Cranford said.

When they emerged from the hotel the rain was still falling. The rainstorm seemed settled for the night. They walked along the boardwalk seeking the restaurant Cranford had spotted on their ride in. They went inside and ate. On leaving the restaurant Trench decided he wanted to go for a drink. Cranford declined to join him and they parted company for the evening. Trench went looking for liquor and a woman. Cranford returned to the hotel to his bed, his dreams and his money.

By six-thirty Cranford and Trench were out of the hotel. They returned to the restaurant for breakfast. It was just after seven when they made their way towards the depot. They had sold off their horses and gear to the owner of Marcos's only livery stable. All they owned was in the saddle-bags they carried. It was enough, as far as Cranford was concerned. He intended to start a new life and he had all he required in his saddle-bags.

It was still raining, though not as heavily as the night before. Now a misty drizzle wafted along the muddy strip of earth that served as Marcos's main street.

The depot appeared deserted, though the office was open and the stove burned brightly. Cranford and Trench stepped inside, dropping their saddle-bags on one of the benches. Trench slumped down beside them. He shook rain from his hat, then began to build a cigarette.

'You want one, Amos?'

Cranford shook his head. He watched Trench silently, thinking that if he didn't have need of Trench's skills, the man's latent violence, he would dispose of him instantly. But Trench, at the present, was an extremely valuable ally.

'Damn clock moves slow,' Trench grumbled.

'It'll get there,' Cranford said.

And it did. The train rolled into the depot right on eight. The engine was a real old hayburner, rattling in every joint and bellowing steam from every seal. Thick smoke erupted from the black-ened stack, drifting like a dark cloud. The engine was hauling a line of stock-cars loaded with bawl-ing cattle. Tacked on at the end of the line was a much-abused passenger coach.

'Thank Christ for that,' Trench muttered. He snatched up his saddle-bags and made for the door.

Cranford followed at a distance, letting Trench go ahead to check the way. Half-way across the loose-boarded, rainslick platform Cranford saw Trench pause, then turn suddenly, throwing out a warning hand.

A cold hand clawed at Cranford's gut. He pivoted slowly, glancing along the platform, peering through the grey mist of rain.

'You son of a bitch!' Cranford spoke so that only he heard.

Frank Angel was standing at the far end of the platform. He was soaked, his clothing muddy and stained, but he looked primed.

'End of the line, Cranford,' Angel called and began to walk towards them.

Cranford let the saddle-bags slide from his hand. As they thudded to the platform Cranford flipped back the skirt of his black coat and reached for the gun holstered on his right hip. He slid the gun free, dropping to a crouch as he levelled the weapon and fired. His bullet ripped up a long wood splinter from the platform. Cranford cursed and fired again. But Angel wasn't there any longer. The Justice Department man had dropped to the platform, sliding his body over the edge on to the bed of the tracks.

'Trench,' Cranford whispered, jerking a hand in the man's direction.

'Yo!' Trench acknowledged, and opened his coat to expose the whip looped around his waist.

Sleeving rain from his eyes Cranford edged across the platform until he was behind a large wooden packing-case standing close to the booking-office wall. He spotted movement down near the wheels of one of the cars and fired. His bullet clanged against a wheel.

'Angel . . . Angel?' Cranford yelled. 'You want to deal?'

'No deals, Cranford. Just you with your hands up and the gun on the ground.'

Cranford quickly reloaded his gun. He was sweating heavily despite the cold rain. He knew that unless Trench could get to Angel it wasn't going to be easy getting out of this one. He had underestimated Angel. It had been a mistake not making completely certain that the man had died back in Liberty. But Cranford hadn't had a lot of time to spare. He'd been too busy getting at the money in the safe. He finished loading his gun. They did say that a man had to pay for his mistakes. Cranford eased back the hammer of his gun. Maybe he could get Angel to pay for them instead. He glanced round, looking for Trench, but the man had vanished. Probably trying to come on Angel from a different direction.

'Angel?' Cranford called. 'There isn't any sense in this.'

There was no reply. Cranford hadn't really expected one. His only reason for speaking had been the hope of distracting Angel while Trench worked his way closer.

'Angel? You can't expect me to quit, man! You know damn well they'll hang me! Man would have to be a fool to give himself up for that.'

Still no reply. Cranford peered round the edge of the packing-case. The rain drifted across the platform and stung his eyes. Cranford blinked. Then he saw a blurred shape moving across the platform. A momentary panic gripped him. Was it

147

Angel? He pawed at his eyes, blinking furiously. In his haste he half-rose to his feet, bringing up his gun at the same time. His finger was tightening on the trigger when his vision returned to normal and he recognized Angel. They fired in the same instant of time. A powerful blow struck Cranford's left shoulder, spinning him off his feet. He banged up against the wall of the booking-office, stumbling awkwardly. As he went down he felt a hot rush of blood streaming down his arms soaking the material of his shirt and coat. Then he hit the wet, dirty boards of the platform, his face rubbing against the splintery wood. He lay, sick and giddy. The pain in his shoulder was terrible. He turned his head and saw the pulsing, bloody hole in his shoulder. A cold sensation washed over him and he knew, without further thought, that it was over. He'd lost and this time there was no way out. He didn't even think that Trench could help.

As far as Angel was concerned Trench was still a threat. He still had the man in mind as he reached Cranford's side, bending to pick up the man's gun and toss it aside. He straightened up, and heard a soft footstep at his back. Angel's body stiffened. Trench! He spun round, gun cocked and ready in his hand. And as he faced about he heard the sharp whistling hiss that could only have come from the whip Trench carried. He caught a quick glimpse of Trench, grinning, his face wet from the rain, standing close to the edge of the platform. Then there was a vicious crack, a blinding burst of pain that engulfed his right hand. Angel's fingers went numb, the Colt dropping to the platform. He felt the hot spread of blood running across his hand.

'You were the first man to escape from my camp,' Trench said. He flicked his arm and the long black lash of the whip arced back to him. 'Kind of sits like a lump in my craw. I mean, a man has his pride to think of – don't he, Angel!'

The arm moved again and the long tongue of the whip snaked forward. It curled across Angel's shoulder, snapping cruelly down his back, laying open shirt and flesh alike. The pain was sharp, bringing forth a gasp from Angel's lips. He fell back, knowing that there wasn't far for him to retreat, and realizing that he was going to have to do something quickly, else he was going to end up like Birdy – cut to bloody ribbons!

'I ain't even got warmed up yet, Angel,' Trench grinned. He was enjoying himself. Having a hell of a time. And he laughed even more when Angel apparently slipped and went down on his knees. Trench contemplated the bowed figure, the sight of Angel's broad, exposed back promising an excellent target. Trench jerked back his arm, bringing the bloody lash back to him. That was when Angel moved, faster than Trench could follow. Angel's left hand came up from somewhere around the top of his left boot, and Trench was certain he saw something flash in the pale dawn light. His mind was still deliberating on what might have caused the flicker of light when the cold Solingen steel blade of Angel's knife penetrated his throat, cutting its way deeply into the tender flesh. There was a second of numbness, then awful, deep-down pain. Trench, still not quite realizing what had happened, released the whip and clamped both hands to the rigid thing protruding from his throat. He began a blind, mindless cry of animal fright and agony, repeated when he became aware of the torrent of blood surging from his throat. He gripped the handle of the slender knife and yanked it free, tearing the wound even more in the process. But he was too late. The damage had been done. He was already beginning to choke on his own blood, coughing raggedly, spewing a pink froth from his jerking mouth. He fell back against one of the stationary cattle wagons. One of his feet went over the edge of the platform and he pitched forward, slamming face first to the platform. Blood spread out from beneath his jerking body in watery fingers, soaking into the soft boards.

Frank Angel climbed to his feet. He retrieved his gun, picked up the knife Trench had dropped and returned it to its sheath in the side of his boot. He turned and saw Amos Cranford, still down on the platform, watching him with vacant eyes. Angel stared at the man for a long moment. Cranford didn't say a word.

Heavy footsteps pounded along the platform. Angel stood and waited for them to reach him.

The local lawman was in the lead. He was a tall, capable-looking man in his early forties. A taut, keen face, browned from a lifetime under the sun. His dark hair was grey-flecked, but that didn't fool Angel. The man was probably as dangerous as the sawn-off scattergun he was carrying.

'You stand right where you are, boy,' the marshal said. He ran a quick eye over the scene, taking in the still figure of Trench and the prone Amos Cranford. Then he glanced back at the tall, rangy young man with the boy's features in a face that bore the experience of a lifetime. 'Appears to me, son, you got some fast talking to do.'

Frank Angel put away his gun.

'Marshal, let me show you something,' he said and reached, with his left hand, for the badge in his belt, thinking that he was having to take the damn thing out so often of late it might be easier to wear it on a length of cord around his neck. 'I think this will do most of my talking for me.'

The marshal took the badge and studied it. He raised his eyes to Angel's face, sighed, and lowered the scattergun.

'So what can I do to help?' he asked, and Angel knew it was over.

As quickly as that.

17

'This report reads like an eyewitness account of a massacre!'

Angel, feeling awkward in a new dark suit, sank back in the leather armchair, and watched the changing expression on the Attorney General's face. Billowing clouds of cigar smoke rose to the ceiling of the spacious room that was the office of the Attorney General, the man responsible for the control of the department which managed all aspects of law enforcement for the United States.

'My God, Frank, did you leave anybody alive down there in Arizona?'

'Only those who weren't doing their damndest to kill me!' Angel replied with rather more force than he had intended.

The Attorney General's eyebrows lifted a fraction, the only indication that he had noticed

Angel's insubordination. He immersed himself in the lengthy report once more, refraining from further comments. After a long and awkward silence the older man put down the sheaf of papers.

'You were sent originally to bring back Harry Culp. First you get mixed up with that mess at Butler's Station and the Reece gang. Then you move on to Liberty and start in on another fracas. To cap it all Harry Culp ends up dead anyway.'

'I hope you noticed that the money Culp took has been returned, sir,' Angel pointed out.

'So has a record of all the dead men involved.'

Angel sat upright. 'Am I right to assume I'm on the carpet over all this, sir?'

The Attorney General made a great ceremony of relighting his cigar. He glared at Angel across the desk.

'You can assume what you like, Mr Angel.'

Anger rose in Angel's face.

'Let me point something out, sir. I didn't go looking for trouble at Butler's Station. The situation wasn't my doing. I just became involved. What was I supposed to do? Ask to be excused because I had pressing business? I don't think I would have got away with it. It was just the same in Liberty. I happened to come along at the wrong time – or right time – depending on how you look at it. I didn't ask to be thrown in jail – sir!'

A hint of a smile touched the corners of the Attorney General's mouth as Angel reminded him

of the incident of his time spent in Liberty's jail
and labour camp.

'No, I must agree there, Frank. You didn't ask to
be put in jail. But you were!' The last words were
delivered with relish. 'Still, it does no harm to see
things from both sides of the fence – or bars in
your case.'

'It's something I won't forget,' Angel said, and
thought: neither will you, you son of a bitch, sitting
there having a quiet chuckle, and I wish that damn
cigar would choke you!

The Attorney General leaned back in his seat,
his face relaxing.

'All right, Frank, we've both had our say. I've
chewed you out because I've been chewed out.
You've had your go at the bone, called me a son of
a bitch under your breath, so let's consider the
matter closed.'

Angel sighed inwardly.

'Thank you, sir.'

'Amos Cranford will be going to trial next week.
I have no doubt that he'll hang. A US marshal is
looking after matters in Liberty until the mess
there is sorted out. It's going to take some time to
uncover all of the details relating to the schemes
Cranford and the late Sheriff Sherman had organized. I've had a report that most of the men in
that labour camp have been set free.'

'A little late for Birdy.'

'Birdy? Oh, the man who helped you. Yes. Pity
about that.' The Attorney-General glanced at a

154

paper he had picked up. 'You'd better take a few days off. By the looks of you a good rest is indicated. But stay in Washington. You'll be required to give evidence at Cranford's trial. It'll be a help to us now that we have Sherman's written confession to use, Lucky it wasn't damaged in the explosion. Good thinking on your part, Frank. In the event it was providential.'

'Sometimes I do use my head,' Angel remarked.

'Yes . . . sometimes,' the Attorney-General conceded. 'Even in the line of duty. Now get out of here and relax. And try and do it without wiping out half of Washington. May I suggest that you consider inviting a certain young woman out for dinner. It would be a personal favour to me, Frank. Miss Rowe has been somewhat agitated because of your extended absence. Go and reassure her that you are sound in wind and limb.'

Angel knew he was forgiven. The Old Man actually giving his blessing to a physical union with Amabel Rowe was comparable with Moses receiving the Ten Commandments – it was no less than an act of God!!! Angel stood up and made to leave before the Attorney General had a brainstorm and changed his mind.

'Oh by the way, sir, I forgot to give you this,' Angel said, dropping a folded paper on the desk.

The Attorney General opened the paper and read it. 'What is this, Frank?'

'Doctor's bill, sir. For medical attention I received in Liberty.'

The Attorney General rattled the paper.

'You expect the department to pay it?'

Angel, half-way through the door, glanced over his shoulder.

'Why, of course, sir.'

'One good reason?'

'Injuries received . . .'

'Yes?'

'. . . In the line of duty . . . sir!' Angel said, and got out fast, before the Old Man found something to throw at him.